Cocos Beckons
The Curse of Yemayá

BRIAN R. LANGHOFF

Foreword by Albert Bouchard of Blue Öyster Cult

Check out

www.cocosbeckons.com

for merchandise, deals, new releases, author appearances,
information, and more…

Published in the United States of America by P3 Press 2021

ISBN: 978-1-7375996-0-9

For information address: *P3 Press.*

Website: www.cocosbeckons.com

P3 Press is a subsidiary of P3 Consolidated Services, LLC—NC, USA

*To my wife, Rebecca, for standing behind me and pushing me to
be greater each day, &
To Albert Bouchard and Sandy Pearlman of Blue Öyster Cult,
whose concept of Imaginos inspired me with the visions that
allowed me to create this story.*

FOREWORD

Brian R. Langhoff first contacted me about this book in early 2020. He is a great fan of my band, Blue Öyster Cult, and a great fan of an album that I had a major part in producing, *Imaginos*. I was one of the founders of BÖC and wrote many of the songs on their most popular albums. On our longest lasting hit, (Don't Fear) The Reaper, I sang, played drums, cowbell, and played a role in the arrangement of the song.

Imaginos was commissioned by Columbia Records to be my first solo record but discord in the record company caused the record to be released under the BÖC name in 1988. In late 2020 I released my own solo version, called *Re Imaginos*, to great acclaim, sales, and chart position that the original failed to achieve.

When Brian first wrote to me, he told me he was writing a book that was inspired by the songs of *Imaginos*. I told him I was interested in reading it. When he sent me a copy, I enjoyed it but I felt some improvements could be made. He was eager to hear my thoughts, so I sent him suggestions. When he sent a revised edition a few months later, I was amazed at how much the entire tale had come together.

I said I would give him my wholehearted endorsement.

The story features strong female characters and is a cultural, continental and century spanning chronicle. This author weaves a captivating, complex and thoroughly enjoyable read.

Albert Bouchard

AUTHOR'S NOTE

In the late-1980s I was listening to a late-night music program on a local radio station in Wisconsin. The guest that evening was none other than the band, Blue Öyster Cult of "(Don't Fear) the Reaper" fame who discussed their newly released album, *Imaginos*. During the interview, the host played a track called "Astronomy" which immediately captivated me. I knew I needed to buy this album. At the time I was in high school and working several minimum wage jobs to save for an education, so money was something I did not spend without a good reason.

The following weekend, my buddy Steven Wilkinson and I headed to the town of Appleton, Wisconsin, and visited one of our favorite music stores. They had a huge selection of albums on the new compact disk storage media. We spent over an hour perusing the racks and titles. I searched for Blue Öyster Cult's new album, but my search was in vain. I settled on a couple of other titles and grabbed a copy of *Simon and Garfunkel's Greatest Hits* along with Pink Floyd's *The Dark Side of the Moon*.

I felt dejected. My hopes had been dashed at the possibility of finding my dream album. Yet, when I approached the register to check out, *Imaginos* was a featured special display. I snatched a copy and admired the cover art through its shiny plastic wrapper.

My friend and I spent the rest of the day goofing around in town before grabbing a meal and driving the 45 minutes back home. Steve had just installed a CD player in his new Dodge Omni hatchback and we chose to play one of his just-purchased albums. I was giddy with anticipation during the ride which seemed to last twice as long as usual.

That evening, I listened to my album three times back-to-back before heading off to bed. Every time I listened to the songs I was overtaken by the band's vivid imagery. I had no idea if the images I was seeing had anything to do with the album, but they were my interpretations of the music and lyrics. For years after that I saw many of the same images every time I listened to the album and a story began to emerge.

Fast forward to the early 2000s while I was dealing with significant stresses in my life. One fall day I was having an especially hard time, so I put in my *Imaginos* album to relax. It had been several years since I had last listened to the album, but on the first note, all the familiar images came pouring back into my consciousness. The story raced through my mind as nearly every detail splayed out before my mind's eye. At that moment I knew what I had to do: my story had to be written.

A few days later we were in a doctor's waiting room for my wife's appointment. I happened to have a copy of the first few chapters I had completed with me. To alleviate the boredom, I offered them to her to read as a distraction while we patiently waited to be called back. Now, my wife loves to read and has hundreds of books in a library I built for her in our home, so I figured that if my story had a chance, she would be able to tell me. She read those few chapters slowly and carefully which is uncharacteristic of her reading style. When she finished, she had tears in her eyes and a puzzled look on her face. She turned to me and said, "You didn't write this. Where did you get it?" I reassured her that I had in fact written the work resting in her hands. She then turned to me once again and asked, "Where's the rest?"

I chuckled and pointed to my head. "In here," I responded, and that is how it all began.

I spent about nine years writing pieces of the story in the limited time I had available. While watching a PBS program one evening I learned about a not-so-famous pirate named Benito "Bloody Sword" Bonito and everything began to click. I started researching the history of Cocos Island and detailing my characters, many of which are based on people I had known over the years who had left an indelible mark on me. I always believed that a strong storyline with engaging characters would be essential to a successful novel. I worked hard to capture the reader's attention with determined and resolute female leads, vivid descriptions, and plenty of plot twists along the journey.

In 2016, I finally made a commitment to myself that I would finish the story and get it published. My daughter and grandson had moved away and I used writing to fill the void they left behind. With a more committed and focused effort, I finished the final details of the manuscript over the next three years.

In 2019, I began a serious effort toward editing my completed work. I was also eager to find an unbiased critique of my work. While browsing the internet late one night, I crossed paths with Albert Bouchard, who'd founded Blue Öyster Cult along with his friend Sandy Pearlman. Together, they created the *Imaginos* concept from the poetry and stories Sandy had written years earlier. I discussed with him my recurring visions while listening to their one-of-a-kind album. He told me some of the history of the band and the origins of the album's material and how it related to the band's name. I also researched the meaning of the album and its songs and was surprised to find that my story paralleled many aspects of the original concept. Albert agreed to review my work as a "loose" interpretation of the album from my own point of view. I excitedly submitted my manuscript to him and after a couple of weeks I got a response. Albert is not a man to pull punches and he pointed out the problems as well as the positive attributes of the story. With critique in hand, I went back to work rewriting large portions of the story and adding three new chapters. Once I completed my work, I sent it back to Albert for his thoughts. In a few days he responded with something along the lines of, "Now that's what I am talking about. Grab the reader and pull them into your world." With his reassurance and unbiased critique I knew I was on the road to something greater than I ever imagined and the *Cocos Beckons* saga became a reality.

Cocos Beckons

The Curse of Yemayá

Route of the Lady Destiny
Key West
Tancun
Cristobal
Balboa
Isla Del Coco
Cocos Island
N

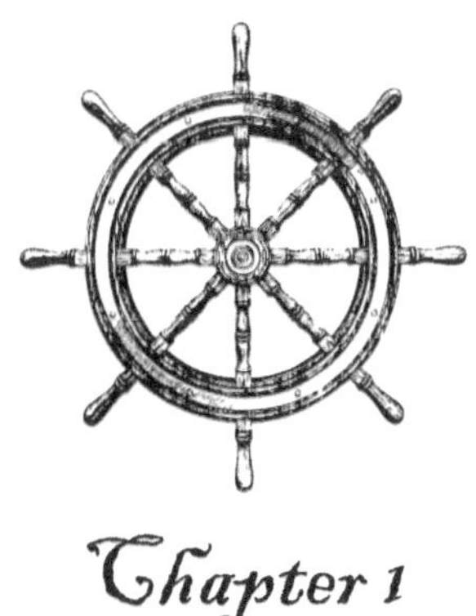

Chapter 1

A FORESHADOWING

1819 A. D.

"The captain is going to get us all killed! He's torturing us by sailing into the bowels of hell," the young dark-haired deckhand whispered, his words rushing out in a mad torrent.

"Why do you say that? You called me to this assemblage to discuss this voyage. This act could put us all at great risk if the captain finds out," came the hushed reply.

"My pardon, Quartermaster. I may have spoken out of turn, but with each passing moment, our torment grows. We have already lost two to their own hands. Most would rather die than deal with this unyielding pain."

"I understand your concerns. I suffer too, but I do not believe that the captain would purposely put us in the path of mortal danger."

The young deckhand looked around at the six gathered. He also peered past the small group to see if there may be others eavesdropping on their clandestine meeting. "When we came on board you said you were here for the crew and would ensure we were treated fairly. We trusted you and we need answers. Now!"

"What do you want to know? I will tell you what I can."

"We want to know what's so important that the captain would travel so far from land in waters that few others would dare travel. Before we can continue to serve on this vessel, we must know where we are going and what we have to gain," said the sandy-haired lad kneeling to the quartermaster's right. He was already a seasoned deckhand and well-regarded by the young crew even though he was only seventeen years of age and could barely grow a proper beard. His confidence and powerful demeanor placed him in a position of natural leadership from the start.

"What are you implying?" asked Arvid, the quartermaster. "I would be cautious of the words you use around here. We may be in a dark corner of the cargo hold, but there are still ears that hear everything. You should trust no one and most especially me. Regardless of your intent, your words could be considered treasonous and place you all in peril."

"My apologies, Quartermaster. It is just that we are all ill and in pain. Our faculties are impaired and we do not always think clearly. We must have some relief from our situation. To faithfully continue with our assigned duties, we must have assurances."

"What kind of assurances?" asked the quartermaster with a raised eyebrow as he craned his neck to face the young man straight on.

"We need to know that this voyage is worth the pain and that we will be properly compensated for our distress. We also need to have assurances that our good health will return," said a third deckhand of the six gathered around. This young man was about nineteen but looked every bit of twenty-five. This was his second voyage and his first on this vessel.

"Son, I can assure you that the voyage will be worth the pain and effort. As your quartermaster, I can tell you that you will be justly compensated upon our return to port. The captain may seem distant and uncaring, but in my experience on this vessel, I have seen that he holds his crew in high regard and depends on them for the efficient operation of his ship. He also pays well, but in return, he demands your unquestioning loyalty, and if needed, you must be prepared to battle in defense of this ship, its crew, and its captain."

"We understand," said the third man. "But why must we suffer so?"

"That question I cannot answer because I do not know. This is my second voyage to this particular location and the last time we were not struck with such anguish and discomfort. I cannot tell you why it is happening, but I can assure you that all hands are suffering." He paused for emphasis. "I am suffering too," he said with a steely and intent stare.

The first deckhand piped in, "I believe that at least the first and second mates are not suffering as we do, and if the captain is suffering, he shows no signs of discomfort."

Just then, they could hear footsteps overhead on the middeck. They immediately ceased their hushed exchange until the footsteps were far enough away that any sounds they made would be covered by the clanking of the rigging and the noises made by the ship passing through the waves.

The second deckhand broke the silence. "Quartermaster, you still have not told us where we are going and why."

"I know, my boy, there are some things I just cannot share with you without placing you at grave risk," Arvid said in a forced but hushed whisper with a touch of gruff vibrato. "You know we are traveling in a generally westward direction. For now, that is all you need to know. We will be arriving within a day and will depart within hours of arriving. If I revealed our destination or even implied its location, it would be considered an act of treason against the captain. He would run me through and dispatch all of you overboard. Trust me that I will do what I can to ensure your safety. I ask that you do not make statements that could imply any inklings of mutinous intent. Those words will ensure that you will not return to port with your limbs intact. The captain will find your cohorts and carry out similar sentences on them without trial or discussion. He will not even allow you to beg for mercy, so remove these thoughts from your minds and do not speak such words again. If you do, there will be nothing I can do for you and I will be forced to carry out the captain's orders to the full extent of his command. Do you understand?"

"Aye, Quartermaster," the first deckhand responded as Arvid stared deeply into his eyes with the sternness and decisive resolve of an eagle on a quest for its next meal.

"Then we will hear no more of this. Trust me and I will do what I can to protect you and assure your safe return to port. Return to your duties and say nothing of this conclave or what we have discussed." Arvid kicked a bilge-soaked rat as it scampered past. It released a fowl scream as it impacted with a nearby barrel. "I will have words with the captain in due time and secure your payment upon returning to port. Prove yourselves on this quest and the captain may request that you stay on board as a full member of his crew. This is your seafaring trial and you are in no position to question authority or make demands. Now, leave me in peace and act as if nothing has transpired here."

The small gathering of young, and mostly inexperienced, crewmen quickly disbanded and went about their appointed roles, leaving the quartermaster to sit in the quiet darkness of the cargo hold to deal with his own afflictions. Two climbed the short ladder to the hatch and emerged from the hold to find the second mate leaning on the main mast. They nodded at him in acknowledgment before they continued about their business. The second mate cast a wary eye on them and picked at his yellow and pitted teeth with a shard of dry timber.

The mighty ship rocked gently in the relatively calm waters of the open Pacific Ocean. Its sails fluttered and billowed in the steady breeze. The tattletales hung loosely as the rigging clanked and banged due to the constant listing motions. Nary a living being stirred in the bright light of the nearly full moon that served as a beacon to their travels. It was an unnerving peace for a vessel accustomed to battle.

Arvid knew why they had come to him with their concerns. He was the oldest crewman on the ship and the only one many could turn to as a father or trusted authority figure. He had hired most of them out of their last port of call. Some were residents of a small fishing port called Salina de la Santa Cruz in Mexico. Some were young greenhorns who could barely endure the hard work and long stretches of time at sea. They had abandoned their posts on the vessels they served or were thrown off and left stranded. Now, they were all ill and in pain and had no one else to turn to in their despair. Sweating profusely, he sat on a cask of heavily fermented spirits. Its contents sloshed to and fro in rhythm with the ship.

The quartermaster's bulky frame was eerily lit by a single candle and the moonlight entering through the slats of the cargo hold cover overhead. Arvid hunched over a barrel containing slabs of dried meat and fish preserved in salt, his scraggly hair and beard unkempt. The putrescent smells around him reeked of the same rum and dead fish that also filled the barrels, punctuated by the pungent odors of urine and feces sloshing in the bilges. *God, would the ringing in his ears ever cease*! In the far corners, he could barely make out the figures of several other crewmen hiding their agony in the dark recesses of the cargo hold. Most had tattered pieces of linen cloth soaked in pitch stuffed in their ears. Some buried their head in their hands or under sacks of flour or grain. Above or below decks it didn't matter—all the crew suffered equal pain.

It was uncommon and unacceptable for any man to show weakness for fear of receiving the captain's wrath at the end of his leather whip or iron rod, but this was no ordinary weakness. Nearly the entire crew seemed to be plagued by a malady of mythical origins and scale. All the affected hands endured a tormenting ringing in their ears that made their heads ache, their stomachs churn, and their bodies quiver uncontrollably, sweating like pigs in the humid heat. There was no escaping the sound as it seemed to originate inside their heads. The thunderous droning noise rang out in their minds like a cathedral bell. Even the "medicinal properties" of the fermented spirits the crew consumed provided little comfort. There was no escape from the horrid sounds, the wretched unwashed bodies, and the stagnant humid heat from hell's bellows.

Only the first and second mates had been spared the torture of the endless ringing that enveloped the crew, so they stood watch in the crow's nest and at the helm. With sadistic laughs, the captain bellowed orders and reveled in the intolerable misery that surrounded him.

Every passing hour increased their torment. They had already witnessed two of the freshly signed crew succumb to the unrelenting sounds as they did themselves in at the end of a rope. Without so much as a grunt, the heartless captain cast their bodies into the sea as fodder for what lurked below.

Arvid was a man of some thirty-two years with nearly half that time spent at sea aboard various vessels of merchants and privateers. He had made this trip once before but never experienced the unholy agony set upon him and the crew. In one hand he clutched a feather quill, and in the other, a vial of black ink. Under his hunched shoulders on top of the rum barrel lay a piece of parchment on which he had scribed a message to his family. This was common practice on extended voyages or when assured peril was expected. The letters would be stored with the crewman's possessions and would be returned to his family should anything happen. He folded the tattered paper neatly into a square. With a groan of agonizing pain and utter exhaustion, he slowly and unsteadily rose to his feet and made his way aft where he located his small footlocker. Each crewman was allowed a small chest to hold their valuables during their time aboard. If they happened to succumb during their time at sea, the chest was to be returned unopened to their family. The stout quartermaster, now hobbled over in pain, had himself delivered too many of these chests to the families of crewmen whom he had served with over the years.

The quartermaster removed an ornate key dangling from a leather cord around his neck. The main body of the key was shaped by intricate brass scrollwork that formed three letters—"W.A.K."—in an elegant script. He placed the end of the key into the lock of the small but strong chest and turned it carefully to release the locking mechanism. Once inside, he emptied its contents. He then looked around to see if anyone could observe his actions, and finding no one, he carefully pulled at a small tab of cloth in the corner to dislodge the bottom panel and reveal a hidden compartment. In this compartment were several pieces of folded linen, a pendant that he normally wore around his neck, some other odd pieces of jewelry, and an assortment of trinkets of seemingly no considerable importance. He carefully placed the letter he had written into the compartment and replaced the panel. After replacing the contents, he locked the chest and returned the key to the safety of his neck.

Arvid wasn't sure exactly why he had written this particular message, but he seemed to be bound by prophecy to do so. For the last month, each slumber was accompanied by a recurring dream that seemed to foreshadow coming events. With each episode, the dreams intensified and became more detailed. Images would flash through his mind as he fought to find rest and recover his faculties. Images of his surly captain brandishing a whip or cutlass; crewmen he had once served with and was currently serving with were being cut down by an unidentified assailant and a young woman with blonde hair and eyes the color of the sea who whispered to him an unintelligible message. At the conclusion of his dreams, he would have a vision of a flash of green light in a setting sun and he would wake soaked in sweat. He struggled to find meaning in these images. They had become part of his routine since visiting a voodoo priestess on a small Caribbean island years earlier while serving as the first mate onboard the vessel of another privateer. She prophesied a glimpse of his future and gave him the gift of foresight which he now believed to be more of a curse than a blessing. The visions were so vivid and real that they drove his actions and guided his hand as he wrote his letter to an unknown recipient.

He was often overcome with feelings of sadness as he lamented his decision to leave the love of his life back home in New England to pursue a career on the high seas. Little did he know that his beloved Hilde was pregnant with his son at the time. The years at sea and constant separation would forever divide them, but alas, she was all he had and the only one he could consider family. Arvid hoped that if anything happened to him, she would at least receive the tokens contained in his small chest so that she might know that he always loved her and longed to be with her.

The quartermaster was one of only a few men a captain could trust on his ship. Being the second in command, Arvid was specifically selected and groomed for the task. He was usually one of the more senior crewmen in age and experience who could carry out the same burdens and responsibilities as the captain, followed by the first mate. This is contrary to most other vessels of the time, but common among the pirate and privateering communities.

He knew the route well; being this was the second time he had made this trip with the captain. He also knew why they would venture to such a remote and isolated place. Those reasons were also why the captain had opted to bring aboard an almost entirely fresh crew before leaving port in Mexico. This fresh crew of young and inexperienced sailors would not know where they were going and could not return to the ship's destination on their own. They made sailing much harder but could be easily manipulated. They would work long, hard hours for an opportunity to make just a few coins and would follow orders blindly out of fear. Once they returned to Mexico, the captain would cast most of them off of the ship and rehire many of his former crew if they were still willing and sober enough to re-enlist with him.

Before his regular crewmen departed in preparation for this voyage, the captain gave each of them a small bag of coins as payment with the promise to double it upon his return if they re-enlisted with him. It was enough to keep them drunk and occupied by whores and games of chance for several weeks. Many would return to benefit from the captain's generous gesture and refill their empty pockets. Those that knew him were aware that beneath the rough exterior, he was a man of his word who valued his trusted crew. He could be cruel, but he paid well, and their raids were usually successful with few injuries or casualties. The captain also knew how to keep secrets. He was not a fool and hid his gains in various locations to deter mutinies and keep his men engaged in trying to secure a larger share of the take.

As quartermaster, Arvid was confident and knowledgeable. But under this oftentimes brutish captain he felt uneasy and many times unsure of his future. It was uncharacteristic for this captain to smile or show any great degree of joy. He was known to be distant and unfeeling as he dealt with the crew, but on this excursion, he had not disciplined a single crewman when they erred or questioned his authority. He even managed a half-hearted smile as they discussed the plans of the day. One could only wonder what the captain's true motives were and what he was hiding. The odd and misplaced actions of the captain induced an uneasy calm over the vessel and crew, making each man leery and guarded.

Climbing the last rung of the ladder onto the main deck, the intensity of the moonlight nearly blinded Arvid. His head began to pulse with an intensity beyond the comprehension of any ordinary man. He stumbled for a moment but soon found his footing and made his way toward the helm. In only a few hours they would arrive at their destination and the next part of this adventure would begin.

At that moment, the captain emerged from his cabin and proceeded up the stairs to join Arvid and the first mate at the helm.

"How are things tonight, Arvid?" the captain inquired.

"Steady sailing, sir."

"Are we still on course for our destination?"

"I am getting ready to check that now, sir."

"Good. When you finish, report your findings to me so that I can plan for our arrival."

"Aye, sir."

The captain turned toward the narrow stairs leading to the mid-deck and returned to the sanctity of his cabin.

Arvid had taken these readings and made the necessary calculations hundreds of times. His results would be undisputed and would ensure their safe arrival. Once he had finished, he put the instruments back into their cases and strode down the stairs to the door of the captain's stateroom on the mid-deck. He took a deep breath and knocked three times.

The word "Enter!" bellowed from within.

"Captain, I have taken the measurements and made a minor course correction. We should arrive within four hours just as the day breaks." Arvid turned to depart the captain's quarters.

"That is good news. We will have the comfort of the waning night's coolness to assist in our tasks. Arvid? Do you have anything else to report?"

Arvid turned around slowly to show proper respect and squarely face his captain. "Yes, sir. Last night we lost two more crewmen to this mysterious malady. They offered themselves as a sacrifice to the sea and sank to their deaths."

"I am not surprised. How many does that leave?"

"Ten, sir."

"That will be enough, provided we do not lose anymore."

"Sir, may I ask you a question?"

"I trust you with my mortal soul, Arvid. You may ask me anything you like, but it doesn't mean I will answer you."

"Sir, why is it that you, the first mate, the second mate, and a boatswain are not affected by the torments that drive the rest of the crew mad? I too am not exempt from this torture."

The captain chuckled heartily. "When we were in battle not long ago and all seemed lost, I made a deal with Yemayá, the Mother of the Sea. I asked her to assist me and spare my life. In return, I pledged myself to her service. The others also made a similar deal. In the end, we won the battle and commandeered this vessel to replace our sinking hulk. I named it *Relampago* to remind me of my obligation to Yemayá and of her mighty power over the sea and storms. For that, I am bound to the sea and obligated to serve Yemayá. Our deals also rendered us immune to the trials of the sea and that is why they remain on board. I will live forever in Yemayá's keep, and I will enjoy the pleasures of our exploits into eternity until she takes me for her own or my obligation is terminated."

"Sir, you call it an obligation. To me, it seems to be more of a deal with the devil and a curse."

"It is all in one's perception, Arvid. We all witness events that may be interpreted in many different ways. It is up to the beholder to determine the true intent of the occurrence and render judgment accordingly. That is how we build and maintain trust among a crew of scoundrels. I see my deal as a blessing. I will live forever with my treasure and will defend it into eternity."

"Aye, sir," Arvid replied in a hushed tone. "I will return to my duties now," he said as he turned and departed the cabin. He was once again momentarily blinded as the moonlight assaulted his eyes and disturbed his faculties. His body became awash in feelings of fear and doubt. Never before was he so unsure about his future. Even with his gift of foresight, he could not see much hope for the coming days. His stomach sank and he began sweating uncontrollably. The morning would bring new unknowns and greater perils, but for now he had a job to do.

Chapter 2

BEHOLD THIS FORBIDDEN PLACE

Arvid rallied the crew as they arrived at a tiny island in the vast ocean. Day had broken only minutes earlier revealing the remoteness of their situation. One glimpse beneath the water's surface and every man knew they were in the middle of the most godforsaken stretch of water the ocean could harbor. Within the beautiful brilliant blue depths exists leviathans that could consume a man in seconds. Dark shadows could be seen gliding slowly and smoothly below their wooden sanctuary; to enter this unholy realm would mean certain and instantaneous death. These monsters had been known to sink small boats and tear the occupants to shreds, turning the tide to blood as a warning to those who would dare tread on this sacred and forbidden land or probe its depths.

The weakened crew brought the ship in dangerously close to an area of shallowly submerged reefs only a few hundred feet from the rocky island. When the captain was content with the position of the ship, he ordered the anchor lowered into the murky depths. The anchor grabbed hold with an abrupt tug as it fought the forces of the erratic currents that pushed and buffeted the ship like a cork in a stream.

Slowly and carefully, the crew lowered a rowboat down the side of the ship to the water below. Two of the most inexperienced crewmen were sent down in the tiny craft. Arvid recognized both of them immediately as two of the instigators of their recent clandestine conclave, the dark- and the fair-haired deckhands. They began receiving bags, chests, and casks of ill-gotten treasure from the crew on deck. One by one they emptied the contents of the captain's hoard from his stateroom into the small boat until it could hold no more.

Once everything was prepared for departure, the captain slid down the side and onto the bow of the rowboat. He was followed by Arvid who turned and received a couple of shovels and a pick from the crew above.

In a deep and demanding tone, the captain ordered the first and second mates to take command of the *Relampago* until he returned. "Send all of the men below and keep them there until we are out of sight. If anyone attempts to disobey my orders, shoot them in the leg and throw them overboard to suffer their fate for disobedience. Be ready to depart when I return and be careful to watch the currents and keep the ship off of the reef. I don't want a damaged ship in these waters," he barked.

"Aye, Captain!" the men responded in unison as they turned and began ushering the men below deck.

Once all men descended below, the captain ordered the two young crewmen to begin rowing the small craft toward a rocky outcropping a few hundred yards in front of the ship. Just past the rocks they beached the boat in an area of flat ground only a couple of yards wide and equally as deep.

The men stepped out of the rowboat onto the tiny sandbar to tie up their craft. They were immediately welcomed by the silent relief from their torturous malady. It felt as if the weight of the world had been lifted from their shoulders and they could once again hear the sounds of nature all around them. But their relief from the thunderous ringing pain was short-lived as the captain ordered them to work in a tone that pierced the men down to their souls.

They pulled a piece of canvas sail material from the pile of sacks and lashed it to two long poles they had chopped from the forest a few feet away. They loaded the entire horde from the rowboat onto the makeshift stretcher and began dragging it behind the captain as he hacked a path for them through the dense brush with his cutlass.

The sun blazed down on their exposed skin like sharp knives. The sweat ran over their faces and stung their eyes as they struggled to maneuver the cargo up a steep incline through the heavy brush. The intense heat of the sun exhausted their energies quickly as every muscle ached with fury. Their legs and arms burned with nagging intensity and spasmed violently from the overwhelming ordeal.

At the top of the incline they found a landing about the same size as the rowboat. They collapsed into tattered heaps. The captain allowed them a few minutes to rest their limbs and regain strength before continuing on his quest.

Just off the edge of the landing a narrow ledge continued around a giant rock about one hundred feet above the jagged rocks and churning ocean below. The captain again used his cutlass to beat back the vines that covered the trail along the ledge as the men grabbed as much as they could carry and followed him. Just on the other side of the rock was another landing about the same size as the last one where they piled the booty before returning to retrieve the rest.

Once all of the captain's goods were assembled on the landing, he had his men tear up some of the sail material into small strips and wrap them tightly around sticks to make torches. Arvid opened one of the casks and the men dipped the torches in whale oil and pork fat. The stench of the rotting substance overpowered them as the sticky goo penetrated the canvas wrappings and cascaded down the handles of the torches. Next, Arvid removed a rock from the satchel he carried and beat it against another rock as he held a torch close by. Sparks sputtered from the impact of the stones onto the torch, which began to smolder. After a few puffs of air from his heaving lungs, the torch was in full blaze.

The captain growled with pleasure as the men ignited their torches. "Grab what you can and follow me." He pulled an area of vines away from a hidden opening in the side of the rocky cliff.

The small band of men stepped carefully through the labyrinth of the cave to an inner chamber. The air inside was cool, stagnant, and damp which gave the tired men renewed energy and welcome relief from the dense morning heat. A small flow of water entered the room through a crack in the stone wall and crossed the floor of the room. The cool liquid felt marvelous on their tired feet as it surged past them to finally disappear into a large hole down to a pool far below. "Be wary, men. If you fall into that abyss, you will not return and will be lost to the sea forever," the captain spouted with a chuckle. "Now go fetch the rest of the treasure as well as the shovels and pick, but leave the three casks behind. We will get those later."

The two young men made several trips out of the damp darkness of the cave and returned with all the treasures in hand. After all the goods were assembled, Arvid pointed out an area along a wall just to the right of the flow of water cascading from the crack in the wall. "Dig there! And be quick about it!" he ordered.

The pick made quick work of the brittle stone as the men dug and hacked out a cavity in the rock face of the cave wall.

Once it was big enough the captain ordered the men to place the treasure inside. While the men stacked the loot inside the fissure, Arvid slipped back outside and retrieved one of the casks, bringing it inside the cave to the men.

"Alright, lads, gather some sand and rock together on this piece of sail," Arvid ordered as he pried open the top of the cask to reveal a powdered ashy substance. He measured out several clumps onto the pile and added a couple of handfuls of water to the mix. "Boatswain, stir this until it is smooth," he said to the young, dark-haired crewman. "And, you, start placing rocks to seal the opening. Use this mortar to make it strong and tight."

It took nearly an hour and a half for the young men to seal up the treasure to the captain's liking. The men sat back in exhaustion and nursed their hands which had been worn raw by the stone and mortar.

The captain turned to them and offered both a pull from his personal flask of rum. "Good job, mates. You have made me proud and for the job you have completed, you will be handsomely rewarded. But, first, you must make assurance to me that I can trust you and that you will not reveal to another living soul what has occurred here or where the treasure is located."

"Aye, Captain!" both men responded with anxious grins.

Arvid began moving cautiously and silently out of the room and back toward the entrance to the cave as the captain continued speaking. He knew what had to happen next. "Well then, we must seal this agreement with a blood oath. Do you agree to my terms?" the captain inquired with a wide grin.

Again the men excitedly replied with, "Aye, Captain!"

"Then who shall be first to offer a bit of his crimson life-blood to seal the deal?" The boatswain raised his hand first. "Good then, laddie. Open your palm to me."

The captain stood and brandished his cutlass. He lined the point up carefully on the boatswain's battered hand to make a small incision. At the last second, the captain thrust his mighty sword into the young man's chest, killing him instantly. Next, he turned to the other crewman who was still lying comfortably on the floor and thrust his sword deep into the young man's neck. Blood flowed from their mortal wounds and the stream that once flowed with clear freshwater now flowed red crimson.

The captain's smile faded as he wiped off his sword on the shirt of the second crewman. He carefully placed the sword back into its scabbard. Finally, he used his booted foot to nudge the men into the hole that passed the water from the stream to the deep pool below. They became his offering to Yemayá.

The captain emerged from the cave just as the torches were dying out. He squinted at the sun hanging motionless in the sky before turning to Arvid. "It is done. I have dealt with a minor inconvenience and secured my fortune in the process. It has been a good day."

Arvid hung his head and whispered quietly, "Aye, Captain."

While the captain was dealing with the task at hand in the cave, Arvid had been placing one of the casks into an area of loose rocks above the cave entrance. He then used the cask of greasy oil to lay a trail of odorous slime from the landing up to the cask.

"Sir, shall we make our retreat?"

"Yes, mate. It is time."

The captain dropped his dying torch in the puddle of gelatinous goo at his feet and began walking along the ledge and back toward the rowboat.

The flickering flames from the torch ignited the trail of oil and grease, which quickly reached the cask embedded in the rocks. By that time, Arvid and the captain were nearly halfway back to the rowboat. They scarcely missed a step as the mighty blast of the gunpowder in the cask ignited and brought down the loose rocks from the hillside over the entrance to the cave, sealing the two innocent young crewmen deep inside their damp and watery tomb.

Arvid stepped back into the rowboat and was immediately greeted by the intense pain induced by the ringing in his ears. He rowed back to the ship as the menacing shadows of the creatures below circled them in anticipation of an error in their judgment. Arvid's head pounded as visions of an uncertain future danced through his mind.

Neither man said a word as they climbed the short rope ladder back up to the main deck and crawled over the railing. The crew hoisted the rowboat onboard and secured it back in its perch.

The captain soon stood at his stateroom door facing Arvid and the crew. "Quartermaster! Raise the anchor and make way. Set a course for our port in Mexico. We need to reclaim our proper crew for our next foray into conquest. I am retiring and do not wish to be disturbed until the morning."

"Aye, Aye, Captain," Arvid replied with a stern and forceful tone and then addressed the crew. "You heard the captain, men. Raise the anchor, set the sails and turn to. We sail back to Mexico. First Mate, you have the first watch. Set your course due east."

The haggard quartermaster retired below deck. The dim light of the cargo hold offered some comfort from the unrelenting pounding in his head and the unholy visions in his mind's eye. He collapsed from exhaustion and fell asleep in a hammock dreading the dreams that were to come.

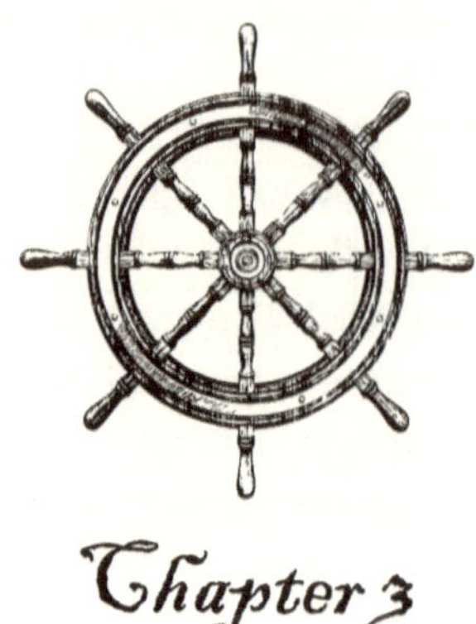

Chapter 3

TWO CAN PLAY AT THIS GAME

The next morning Arvid woke well before sunrise to take readings on the positions of the stars and verify their course back to port. The humidity was already becoming unbearable, but he found some comfort in the diminishing intensity of the ringing in his ears.

He reviewed the charts and plotted their present course on the upper deck near the helm. "Helmsman, turn ten degrees to the starboard and hold your course."

"Aye, Quartermaster," came the response.

Just then the captain emerged from his stateroom. He stood on the deck and stared into the sun as it began to creep above the horizon. He stretched his arms and back and grunted as his joints cracked and popped. "It is going to be a beautiful day," he commented as he turned and cast a sly grin toward the helmsman and Arvid.

The captain walked toward the cargo hold and opened the hatch as he did each morning. He made his way down the ladder to the cask of dried meat. He pulled out a couple of handfuls of the bitter meat and began tearing off pieces with his gnarled teeth, gnawing the tough jerky with obdurate intent as he surveyed his surroundings.

Arvid made his way back down to the mid-deck and met one of the young men he had secretly conversed with just a day and a half earlier. He nodded to the crewman in acknowledgement and shook the young man's hand. As they shook hands, Arvid slipped a small piece of parchment into his grip. The deckhand momentarily flashed a look of astonishment as he met his quartermaster's eye. Arvid cast the young lad a brief wink and whispered to the startled mariner, "Keep it safe. Keep it well. Take me home." They broke their grip and continued in opposite directions. The crewman palmed the scrap of parchment and ran his finger over the surface. He could feel the outline of an object embedded in its folds. Cautiously and without drawing attention, he placed it into a small leather satchel he carried around his neck and went about his duties.

A moment later the captain emerged from the cargo hold and glared at Arvid. "Quartermaster! We are taking on water. We must have impaled the hull on the reef while anchored at the island. Take the rowboat and inspect the port side of the hull near midship for damage and report."

"Aye, Captain! Men, pull in the sails and ready the rowboat with haste!"

The men made short work of lowering the sails and removing the rowboat from its perch, swiftly setting it over the port side. Arvid lowered himself down into the boat using a short, thick rope and grabbed both oars before rowing the craft along the length of the ship. He made one pass toward the bow and then let the ship slowly slip by with its last bit of preserved momentum. Arvid inspected every visible inch that he could from his vantage point. For all of his efforts, he could not detect any damage to the ship. It appeared to be as pristine as the day they left port in Mexico over a week earlier and this is what he told the captain.

"Look harder, damn you! We cannot lose our ship to the briny deep. There has to be something there."

"Sir, maybe I should inspect the inside of the hold myself to determine the possible location of the damage?" Arvid noticed a frantic tone creep into his voice.

"Very well, but first make one more pass along the hull on the starboard side and complete a survey of the full length of the ship."

"Aye, sir," Arvid sighed and began rowing the small craft around the perimeter of the ship, conducting another thorough survey as he was ordered.

Once he had completed his inspection, he rowed the boat back to the place where the rope was dangling over the side so he could return to the main deck. He tossed a small line to a crewman standing above to keep the boat in place. Next, he grabbed the heavy rope and pulled heartily to heave his body back up to the main deck. As he tugged at the rope, it gave way and he fell back into the boat, nearly falling overboard into the steel blue depths and wracking his back against one of the protruding oar locks.

The figure of the captain appeared overhead. He trained an empty gaze on his quartermaster who writhed in pain below. "What have you to report, Quartermaster?"

In labored tones, Arvid responded, "Nothing to report, sir. The hull appears to be intact with no visible damage. It may be a piece of loose chinking between the planks."

"So you have found nothing…then you have failed me."

"How do you mean, sir?" said Arvid with a terrified gaze.

"You have failed me and you have now become a liability. Farewell, my friend. We will pass your possessions along to your beloved Hilde." At that instant, the captain pulled a pistol and fired a single shot at Arvid. The blazing hot lead ball penetrated the side of Arvid's abdomen. It was not a mortal injury, initially, but he knew that the wound would fester and infection would soon render him in a fatal state. Knowing the skill of the captain, he surmised that the placement of the shot was intentional and meant to cause the most intense suffering possible.

The first mate sneered at him with a cold, callous grin and threw the thin line that was holding the rowboat in place back at Arvid, allowing it to dangle freely. After a moment he stalked away and returned to his duties. The rowboat drifted slowly away from the ship as he could see the men hoisting the sails.

Arvid lay sprawled out across the floor of the boat twisting in pain. His wound bled and oozed uncontrollably and his stomach churned with an unsettling sickness. Sweat poured from his body. The hot sun baked his exposed and weathered skin. He had nothing to protect him from vulgar rays except a thin linen shirt and tattered britches. On the horizon, Arvid could barely see the mast of the *Relampago* as it crept out of sight and away from his grasp.

Now he was utterly alone. Only the occasional gull offered any companionship or comfort to him in his tormented state. He had no food, no freshwater, no medical supplies, no shelter, no instruments to guide his way, and no hope for survival.

Every second of excruciating pain felt like a fortnight. He could feel the life flowing from his battered body as the bottom of the boat began to slosh with his vital bodily fluids. He tried to position himself for a better view of his surroundings in hopes that he could glimpse another vessel or spit of land, but he knew these waters well and any hope for rescue was a wasted effort. He was too far from the island and the mainland was even further. There wasn't another piece of land to be found for hundreds of miles. This was why the captain chose the island to hide his stash. Any man trying to find it without knowledge of its actual location was doomed to failure and near-certain death.

Arvid accepted his fate, but that didn't mean he was going to give up on any possibility of survival. The only thing he could do at this point was to try and muster enough energy to row his boat in a direction that might place him into a current shared by another vessel.

Every movement sent twinges of pain coursing through his body like red hot pokers. He was able to make three full strokes of the oars before the pain became too intense to tolerate. It became instantly apparent that this was a fruitless, futile effort, and a waste of valuable energy.

For nearly eleven hours Arvid lay in a fetal heap in the blazing intensity of the tropical sun under a cloudless sky. His glowing tormentor was now beginning to make its final appearance of the day. He held up his hand at arm's length to measure how far above the horizon the sun lay. *Three fingers. That's about 45 minutes to sunset. Finally, I can find relief from the inferno of daylight.*

He once again removed the bloodied linen cloth of his shirt that was covering his wound to inspect the damage. The wound no longer bled, but it uncontrollably oozed clear liquid with pulsating regularity. He was certain that within hours he would meet his demise in the cool silent night. The bile and clear fluids running from the jagged hole left by the lead shot meant that he had significant internal damage and if dehydration did not kill him, infection soon would.

He wiggled and inched his way up to get a better view of the setting sun. By now the brilliant orange orb touched the horizon and in less than two minutes it would disappear completely. He gazed at his blazing tormentor until the last second. Out of habit, he placed his hand on his chest over the place where the key to his precious footlocker once hung. Foresight told him that it was in safe hands and his Hilde would soon know of his fate. He stared vacantly at the horizon just as the sun winked its final goodbye. As the final sliver of light disappeared, Arvid saw an intense flash of green light, but this time there was no waking up from a dream to start a new day.

Only a few thoughts filtered through his dying mind. *My premonitions have come true. Members of the crew are dead at my hand due to my failure to protect them. My friend and captain has betrayed me. Perhaps he knew of the clandestine meeting with the crew, maybe he was overtaken by greed and love of treasure and wished to gain my share, or maybe I knew too much and could no longer be trusted. Now I am left alone to die in this place of emptiness and despair. My hope is gone and Odin has blessed me with a wink from his eye in the green light of a setting sun. All is lost but the sweet death itself.*

Arvid slid back onto the floor of the boat to gain some degree of relief from the intense pain of his wound. He closed his eyes for a brief moment. Suddenly the peace of the ocean was disturbed by the sounds of scratching and tapping. When Arvid opened his eyes he expected to see a gull resting its wings as it perched on the edge of his tiny oasis, but to his surprise, his gaze was met by a pair of black ravens. "What are you doing way out here?" he whispered to the birds as they exchanged stares. His ebony guests made no sounds and remained perched on the edge of the boat observing his inevitable fate.

The minutes became hours. The stars twinkled and danced to entertain his final moments. The full moon bathed the world in soft blue light as the mysterious duo stood motionless before the softly glowing orb. In the distance, he could hear the vaporous expulsions of whales gasping for breath as they prepared to dive and hunt.

Arvid managed to reach his bloodied hand over the side of the boat and drop it into the sea. The impact caused the water to glow a brilliant blue-green from the bio-luminescent plankton riding the currents. With every movement he made and every ripple that besieged the boat, the bio-luminescent sea life glowed with greater intensity until the entire area around his tiny craft was flooded in magical light.

He could feel the life leaving his body. The end was not far off now and he was ready to surrender to the whims of Yemayá. With his last ounce of energy and dying breath, Arvid yelled to the sky above, "Odin, I have seen your light. I welcome your messengers and I will soon see your face in the stars. My greatest regret is that my love does not know of my undying love for her. I will serve you always, but I ask that you grant me revenge against my captain." Arvid closed his eyes and slouched down to await his final fate.

Arvid's final thoughts turned to the memories of his beloved Hilde back in New England, whom he had not seen in some four years and whose touch he would never know again. A tear formed and slowly trickled down his cheek. An immense peace overcame his body and the world seemed to melt from around him. Through his closed eyelids, he could still see the light of the full moon. The light was soft and calming. He was awash in the glow of bio-luminescence and moonlight. He relaxed into his weakened state and waited for the inevitable.

A few seconds later he could sense that things were changing. The ravens that kept him company and escorted him to his final destination cawed loudly and departed on a cool passing breeze. The light penetrating his eyelids began to intensify and transform into a bold green. He managed to barely crack open his eyes to glance at the cause of this luminous transformation.

As his eyes opened to narrow slits he could see only intense green light all around his world which had fallen completely silent. His pain seemed to be fading. He was sure this was the end.

"Wilhem, Son of the Sea. Bearer of foresight and plagued by frightful visions in the night, I have heard your call and ask you to bear witness to me this night," came a voice booming through the light. "My trusted messengers, Huginn and Muninn have carried your plea to me."

"I hear you, Odin."

"Wilhem, I will grant you your dying wishes, but you must remain in my service until you have atoned for your actions and earned entrance into your next life in Valhalla."

"I understand, Lord Odin. What are your terms?" Arvid responded in his mind since his lips no longer responded to his motor commands.

"My terms are simple. When your mortal soul departs your earthly remains, you will serve me as I command. You will be a messenger from the other side and a protector to your lineage. You will exist in neither world, but you may still influence the future."

"But, Lord Odin, my beloved and I have not borne any offspring. I have no lineage."

"You are mistaken, my son. You left your beloved while she carried your child all those years ago. He bears your name and continues your bloodline. It is from his loins and the continuation of your bloodline through the generations that you will find relief from your obligations to me."

"Please explain my duties so that I may make my decision in good conscience and with clear understanding."

A soft breeze blew past Arvid as his pain completely fell away and his energy returned. With renewed vigor, he sat upright in the boat and opened his eyes wide to peer into the green light of Odin's eye. He raised a hand to his face to block some of the intensity and make the light more bearable to his unadjusted eyes.

"Wilhem, my son, I will grant you the ability to once again

see your beloved, but you may not touch her. You will be allowed to visit her and your descendants whenever you like and
through this influence, you may assist and guide your lineage
to guarantee their paths are pure of purpose. I will grant you
your revenge, but it will require a trinity from your bloodline
to dispatch the evil your captain harbors. With the success of
your revenge, he will lose claim to the treasure. The third of
your trinity will be allowed to collect only your share of the
treasure but must pay a price in exchange. Just as your dreams
have foretold, your great-great-granddaughter will fulfill this
trinity and assist you to free your wandering soul. Just as your
captain is obligated to serve Yemayá, you will serve me. On
a night like this one many years from now, you will meet the
revenge you desire. Only one of treacherous blood may undo
the captain's curse and dispatch his bridled soul. With that final
act, your service to me will end. You and the others joined in
your family trinity will be granted admission into Valhalla, for
your revenge comes at a price of sacrifice. Do you agree with
these terms?"

"My greatest wish is to see my beloved once more. I would
like to watch my family grow, know my son, and have my descendants benefit from my influence, but I do not agree with
the terms you are implying for my great-great-granddaughter's
fate. I understand the terms. They tear at my heartstrings and
fill me with deep sadness."

"Wilhem, with every good, comes bad; with every positive, there's a negative; with every life taken for evil, one must
be given for good. It is how the world maintains balance. You
wish to end the terror of a murderous pirate, but there must
be a sacrifice to offset the deed."

"And what if I refuse to accept these terms?"

"For the lives you have allowed to be unjustly taken, and
the deeds you have done, you will be punished and serve out

eternity in isolated torment. Your empty shell will rot in this boat to be picked clean by the birds of the air while you watch. You will then wander the earth in solemn isolation, never again knowing another's touch or hearing any words of comfort. You will be utterly alone for all eternity with your thoughts and the memories of the things you have done which will torment your sleepless existence and drive you into everlasting madness. You will roam without peace and without a chance of earning your way into Valhalla. You will forever be a lost and lonely tortured soul in a vast and empty universe void of warmth or a cool breeze."

"So I am to assume that I have no choice in the matter?"

"You have a choice, Wilhem. There must be a sacrifice; whether it's yours or your descendants' matters not to me. You may accept my offer to serve me and earn your entrance to Valhalla at a price or forever exist in a state of agonizing loneliness tormented by your memories and without your revenge."

"I understand, Lord Odin. I have made my choice. I choose to serve you so that I might know my family and feel love even though I will not feel love's tender embrace. I will defend the world against the evil of my captain and forbid him the pleasure of his treasure. Aided by the sacrifices of my family, a trinity from my seed will rid this life and the afterlife of a great tyrant to break his curse. This trinity will then cross over to join you in Valhalla where we will find peace. To this, I solemnly swear that I will forever be your humble servant."

With that, Arvid slumped back into the boat. Though his body had failed minutes earlier, he could still see the light as it dimmed to reveal the full moon in all its glory. He could feel himself become weightless as his life force escaped its worldly bindings and became one with the heavens and a guide to his bloodline. He now existed only as a ghostly force for good, known only to the world by his name. Arvid would appear as a shadow passing through the corner of his descendants' sight, as a brief image hiding in the background of images in a mirror or calm pool, or a cool ghostly pale mist that rides the ocean breezes. He was no longer of this world or the next. He was a being of pure energy that traveled between worlds in the smallest crevices of time and space where only imagination and fantasy usually reside. His only companionship would be Huginn and Muninn, the messengers. They would relay orders to Arvid as he transcended time toward an inevitable end; atoning for his actions as a servant of Odin.

Chapter 4

FALLING IN LOVE

The 2000s

Approaching her mid-thirties, Rachel Kristiansen played by her own code of conduct. Although she liked a strong drink after a long hard day, she also knew in order to survive, she had to stay alert and keep her wits, so one or two were always her limit. She wasn't much for socializing with the local men at the pubs and preferred the solitary life with the things she loved best; time with Gramma Gwen and fishing.

She was a tall, slim, muscular woman with an angular face from years of a hard life in the open air on the sea. She kept her long blonde hair pulled back through her ball cap where it fell against her back and shoulders like a pristine shroud, flowing in the wind. In a strong gust it would crack like a whip. Her skin was fair and free of blemishes except for a scar on her chin which she received when a mooring line broke causing the "bitter end" to whip back, grazing her chin and gashing it open. Her eyes were the bluest blue and when she stood in front of the sea they seemed to disappear as if part of it.

Everything about Rachel tells a passerby she is a child of the sea. Her life was spent in Gloucester, Massachusetts, with her family. Her father, Paul, was a fisherman his whole life and though he barely had an eighth-grade education he was able to raise a family, pay the bills, and provide for their needs even in the worst of times. They didn't have much but they were happy.

Like his daughter, Paul's face was also hardened by the sea, yet he had a softness in his nature, making him pleasant to be around. Of average height with a strong muscular build, Paul was known to have a temper. When he was angry his gaze became dark and piercing and could drain the life from those who had the misfortune of meeting it. Yet, for those who knew him well, they knew him as a kind, spiritual, generous, and caring man who loved his family as much as the sea and would sacrifice anything to protect them.

A study in contrasts, Rachel's mother, Elizabeth, was a quiet, well-mannered, elegant woman who had the face of an angel and alabaster skin that glowed when the sun shone upon it. Her petite figure was both curvaceous and strong, making her the envy of the community. Her hands were as delicate as fine porcelain without a scratch or blemish and she kept them well-groomed and manicured. She was the daughter of the town's former mayor and had been raised with the finer things and the best education in Europe. She cooked, cleaned, and took care of their small stone home which lay mere feet from the docks. Elizabeth was never seen without a smile on her face or a song on her breath. She loved to sing and would sometimes make up her own love songs if she wasn't singing some sea shanty or Irish bar song. She seemed an odd match for such a man as Paul

Kristiansen, but they were destined to be together from the start.

Paul was already a seasoned fisherman when he met Elizabeth in the early 1970s. One evening he was standing on the dock coiling lines for a new net as the sun was beginning to set. Elizabeth had walked down to the docks after dinner. She did this often as she loved the smells wafting up from the sea on the evening air and the feeling of the sun beating down on her face as it winked away its final appearance and displayed its glory in the colors that danced on the horizon. This evening was to be no different from any other as she walked past Paul to the end of the pier and he barely glanced at her as he concentrated on his task at hand.

Elizabeth stood there for some time listening to the gulls gorging on the leftovers from the day's catch. She closed her eyes and let the breeze wash over her as her dress gently rustled against her legs. The sun was a little cooler than usual this evening and as she lifted her eyes she noticed the colors above her head danced in a way reminiscent of the northern lights she had seen years earlier when she had attended boarding school in Edinburgh. It was a fine August evening and all was well with her world.

As she stood on the pier gently swaying in the breeze, she thought of nothing except the tranquility around her. This was her nirvana and it gave her peace.

In an instant, a strong wind raced around her catching her off guard; she stepped back to regain her balance as she swayed on her heels. Another step back and she found herself in a pile of ropes. Now past the point of no return, with the ropes tangled around her ankles, she tumbled into the chilly waters. Elizabeth managed only a small yelp as she fell, but it was enough. She gasped for a final breath as she was pulled under by the weight of the heavy waterlogged lines.

Paul, who had been working only a short distance away, heard the woman's yelp and subsequent splash. Instinct allowed him no control over his actions. He sprang from his seat on the wooden crate, ran to the end of the pier and dove into the water after Elizabeth. Reaching for her outstretched hand he found it once and lost it. Twice more he grazed her arm but couldn't catch hold. Finally, as he was nearing the end of his breath, he found her hand and gripped on tightly. As her body went limp, she stopped struggling and the ropes fell away. She was free!

He struggled to swim to the surface with Elizabeth's lifeless body in tow. They sprang to the surface and Paul gasped for air. He pulled Elizabeth up a ladder and onto the pier. He forced the water from her lungs by compressing on her chest. He took a deep breath and placed his mouth over hers. He filled her lungs with his life-giving breath. Nothing! He did this four more times and finally, on the fifth breath, her back arched and she violently coughed. More water flew from her colorless lips as she blinked her eyes and tried to grasp the reality of the situation. The color flooded back into her cheeks as she realized that she had survived, but only by the grace of God and with the assistance of a stranger who happened to be working on the docks.

Once more, her eyes opened slowly and then shut again. Her breaths came raggedly and her coughing began to subside. Paul picked up her trembling body, cradling her close in his strong arms. She could feel his warmth and the beating of his heart against her. It gave her comfort as he carried her, shivering and shaking, home to her family.

He knew who she was because in this town everyone knew everyone else. Many a man fought to gain Elizabeth's attention. Her father met them both at the front door when he saw Paul carrying her up the short walkway to the porch.

Paul carried Elizabeth's limp body up the stairs, keeping step behind her father as he led the way. He cautiously entered her room and placed her gently onto the bed. To see a man of such stature and strength move with such grace and purpose was not to be overlooked.

At that moment something happened. It was one of those moments that people dream about but never actually believe it can happen. She lay there resting and Paul could see her chest rising slightly, the image of her ample breasts barely perceptible through her thin, water-soaked dress. His heart was pounding, and he felt flushed. Paul turned, blushed slightly, and began to leave the room. On his way out, Elizabeth's father stopped him and grasped his arm. Paul turned slowly toward her father, who choking back tears, whispered, "My son, you are always welcome in our home and our gratitude will be forever with you."

The next evening, after he returned from the day's fishing expedition, Paul checked on Elizabeth. He joined the family for dinner and ate heartily. After dinner, he asked Elizabeth if she cared to go for a walk and with her father's permission they left the house. They walked along the docks and past the boats moored nearby, listening to the gentle rhythm of the waves lapping against their hulls.

The duo said nothing as they leisurely strode on the wharf. People who lived their lives outdoors know the value of silence and in listening to what the world has to say. The night sounds played ballads to their ears as the rocking boats provided the bass and percussion. The moon shone brightly on Elizabeth's perfect ivory skin which glowed with a pale blue hue. Paul reached up and touched her shoulder and he could see the goosebumps appear on her delicate skin. He placed his jacket around her chilled shoulders and she turned to face him. In a voice as soft as a dove's call she said,

"I did not get a chance to thank you for saving me. I owe you my life. Thank you." She kissed him gently on the cheek. She blushed briefly as she looked down in shyness. They turned back toward the sea with Elizabeth cradled once again in Paul's strong, yet tender embrace.

Paul and Elizabeth were married on the first anniversary of Elizabeth's fateful fall. They moved into Paul's mother's historic stone home near the docks where Elizabeth could watch the ships come and go. The home had stood the ravages of time for well over a hundred years. It was built by Gwen's great-grandfather Wilhem for his beloved Hilda in the early 1800s. In Gramma Gwen's cozy home, Elizabeth could feel safe as she waited and watched for her brave fisherman to return to her. She could burst through the front door and rush to him when his boat moored at the pier.

Nearly a year after they were married, they had a beautiful daughter. Rachel Ann Kristiansen was born on a blustery night as a storm swelled and the sea crashed. It was a long, difficult labor and after nearly twenty hours an exhausted Elizabeth cradled the newborn in her arms as she drifted off to sleep.

The next morning, Rachel lay crying in her cradle. Paul picked her up and carried her in for Elizabeth to nurse. He entered the room where there was an eerie quiet. He approached Elizabeth's bed and sat on its edge, but Elizabeth did not stir. He reached down and kissed her cheek and found it cool. Her color seemed to have faded as well. Her normally alabaster skin appeared dull gray. Her eyes were closed, and she smiled slightly. He grasped her hand and found it cold and lifeless to the touch. He said nothing more. He placed his head on her chest and wept only a single tear.

Elizabeth was buried on a Tuesday. The day was cold and overcast. Paul had Rachel cradled close to him for warmth as he placed a single rose on Elizabeth's grave. He turned to leave when the clouds broke and the sun's rays beat against them both with an intensity he had not felt before. The sky was ablaze with colors and the birds began to chirp and sing. It was as if Elizabeth, in her own way, was telling them both that things would be all right and that they could be strong without her.

Chapter 5

A PRICE TO PAY

Paul spent as much time as he could with Baby Rachel. Elizabeth's parents took care of her while he was out to sea and Gramma Gwen worked in the cannery. They introduced her to a structured and well-managed life while making sure she received a good education. On the day of her eighth birthday, Paul began teaching her all that she would need to know to be a good fisherman. Elizabeth's parents had greater plans for their granddaughter, but Rachel shrugged off the strict regimented lifestyle of her grandparents for something more free and exciting. She took to her father's work as if she had always known it.

By the time she was ten, Rachel was joining her father at sea when she wasn't in school or spending time with Gramma Gwen. She had learned to read the sea and work the nets. She could handle the fish and feared very little. Rachel knew the sea as well as her father and some would say even better.

On the day of her eighth grade graduation, Rachel beamed with pride. The day was warm and sunny and that evening after her father returned from the sea, they would attend the graduation ceremony; she would be on her way to high school. She did not go with her father that day as she had things to do before the ceremony.

As the day's hours came to a close, Rachel's excitement swelled. She could barely contain herself as the minutes passed while she maintained her gaze through the window, scanning the harbor. Her smile beamed from her face like a lighthouse on a clear night and her heart pounded with anticipation of her father's return. It was about 6 p.m. and her father should be rounding the bend any second on his way to the pier. The clock began to chime. She heard it ring once, twice, then a third time. It rang a fourth time but not the fifth or sixth. She turned from the window and walked to the clock on the fireplace mantle. She examined it carefully and noticed it had stopped running. The pendulum of the regulator clock had stopped swinging. She grabbed the ornate key and began to wind the clock's spring mechanism but when she restarted the pendulum it still would not swing. She tapped on the clock face cover gently and then on the top.

Rachel turned away from the clock toward the window just as the sun began its final trek toward the horizon. A huge wall of menacing clouds was closing in on the small town. Rachel's heart sank. Her father was out in that storm. She feverishly scanned the harbor from the breakwaters to the horizon with an old set of binoculars. She searched intensely but could not detect any sign of her father's boat.

By 6:30 the full force of the storm had come ashore. Her father still had not returned. Rachel did not attend her graduation.

For a day and a half, the storm raged. On the afternoon of the second day, the sky suddenly cleared. One by one the remaining fishing vessels began returning to port after their ordeal. By that evening all but three boats had returned.

Rachel now understood the meaning of the four chimes and the stubborn clock. The clock had chimed once for her father and once for each man of his crew. It had stopped at the very moment when their lives had ended.

Although no one had confirmed the loss of her father's boat, *Lady Destiny*, Rachel knew its fate. Three days later a single life preserver washed ashore about ten miles away.

The preserver was brought to Rachel and her family and they were told that all hope was lost for her father's return.

In a small ceremony, Rachel and her family laid to rest the one piece of her father that she had. The life preserver was placed in a small grave, and at age thirteen Rachel forever closed the book on her life with her father.

Everyone knew the risks but no one talked about them. Nobody thought it would happen to them. Life was precious and no one in this town took it for granted. These sad rituals happened far too often and many in this town were grieving, but everyone knew it was the way of the sea and the life of the fisherman. The sea gave up its treasures but at a cost. For every blessing, there has to be a sacrifice and for every joy, a sorrow. This was how the sea maintained balance and ensured none took her for granted. A mistress, a temptress, a demon, and a provider; the sea is all these things; sometimes all at the same time. Now all Rachel had was a memory and a monument in town that was dedicated to those who had lost their lives doing what they loved.

Chapter 6

SOMETHING IN THE AIR

"Hello, honey!"

"Hello, Gramma," Rachel called as she walked up the narrow stone path to her grandmother Gwen's small cottage.

"So, how was your take this trip, Rachel?"

"We did well. We pulled forty tons in three hauls."

"That's good. Where are the girls?"

"They might come over later. They wanted to get cleaned up and grab a couple of burgers and beers at the Four Winds Tavern. They get tired of boat food." Sandwiches and coffee will work miracles at sea, but Rachel understood the joy of someone else preparing a meal and being able to eat it in peace on firm ground. Rachel leaned in and kissed her grandmother on the cheek and gave her a hug before turning to enter the cottage.

Gramma Gwen was by no means a frail person. She had an impressive physique from years of hard work at the cannery, preferring jeans and flannels over a skirt and blouse any day. At 72 and of medium height, her manicured hands aged faster than her face with its powerful Norwegian features. Her only wrinkles were her crow's feet because she loved to smile so much. Gwen hadn't cut her hair in twenty years and she pulled her long silver locks back in a ponytail like her granddaughter. She always said, "Like Sampson, my hair gives me strength." She joked that if her hair was properly braided, she believed she could use it as a mooring line. Rachel loved to brush her grandmother's long locks in the evenings when she was home. It brought a quiet calm to the whole house and the weight of the day could be felt melting away. Gwen never had a driver's license, so she walked or rode her bike wherever she needed to go. Many times, she carried a cane but didn't need it. Some speculate that she used it to ward off over-aggressive suitors. Clean living and strong convictions are what she claimed to have kept her young all these years. Her calm, quiet demeanor meant she rarely needed to show her power, and everyone knew she was one woman who wouldn't leave this world without a fight.

Gwen's two-story home was a quaint, yet strong structure. Built in the early 1800s and remodeled countless times since, it had proven that it could withstand the tests of time. At barely more than 1000 square feet, it was cozy, warm, and tastefully decorated in a nautical theme like most homes in Gloucester, with rich dark woods, and paint colors of navy blue, burgundy, and beige to reflect the rich traditions of the families that have lived there for so many years.

The home was constructed primarily of stone with a sturdy timber roof and cedar shingles. When the wind blew you scarcely heard a whisper of the torrents raging outside. The only indication of any harsh weather was the occasional clacking of the three loose shingles at the back corner of the house near the kitchen, much like a bird pecking at a glass window.

In the winter, Rachel's grandmother kept a fire going in the fireplace with a pot of water on the stove for tea. The house always smelled of cinnamon and spices, yet rarely did anyone in the home bake. The sweet scent of vanilla also occasionally drifted down the narrow stairs as if a strange spirit was trying to bring a feeling of contentment to a weary soul after a long day. The one thing that can be said about this house, like so many of the other old homes in the area, was that it has spirit, or as some would say, "spirits."

Sometimes, Rachel would walk down the stairs ever so quietly, trying not to make the old stair treads creak and moan under her steps, just so she could listen to her grandmother as she worked in the kitchen or sat in her favorite rocking chair, peacefully knitting in front of the window overlooking the harbor. Oftentimes, Rachel heard her grandmother talking as if carrying on a conversation with an old friend. When Rachel approached the corner of the kitchen, the voices faded away and her grandmother acted as if she had merely been waiting for Rachel to arrive for breakfast. Many times, she would claim that she was just singing some old nearly forgotten song from her childhood while she chewed the end of an old corn cob pipe that had never seen a match.

On one such occasion, Rachel heard her grandmother talking to someone and repeating the name Arthur. Rachel knew immediately that Arthur was Gwen's dear grandfather who had died many years before. *So how could this be so?* Gwen had had a very close relationship with her grandfather, and was frequently found in his company when she was a child. Rachel believed that this was just Gwen's way of dealing with the many years without her dear grandfather and the loneliness from the loss of her husband many years ago. It was a way to make the house feel a little less lonely and to reminisce about the many happy days behind her. Sometimes, she believed her grandmother was asking Arthur to watch over her granddaughter while she was at sea and to make sure she made it home safely. It seemed that after these ghostly conversations Gwen was happier and more at ease. It also seemed that it was at these times that the pleasant smells of vanilla would be strongest, but again, no source could be found to explain the sweet aroma.

Arthur had enlisted in the navy and been assigned to a ship at the end of World War I. As the war was winding down, the battles still raged on and his ship was hit by enemy fire. Arthur, unfortunately, had been at the wrong place at the wrong time, and one round slammed through the side of his frigate and blew the bulkhead inward, peeling the steel back like a sardine can buckling the deck plates. One of these pieces of steel rolled back and threw Arthur into a hatch door. The impact of his back hitting against a dogging handle broke his spine just below his neck, killing him instantly. Had he made it a few more weeks, he would have been home to care for his family; especially his young granddaughter Gwen, who was working hard to get good grades in school and help around the home.

On this evening, after Rachel had taken a shower and satisfied her hunger with a big bowl of her grandmother's lobster bisque, she went into the den to sit with Gwen. She picked up the remote and began surfing the channels like a madwoman on a mission, catching a rare word or faint image as it passed in a blur of electronic light. After traveling through the labyrinth of channels three or four times, she finally turned off the TV and put down the remote in a huff.

Rachel sat in the dim glow of the evening light, watching the waves roll and churn in the harbor with a rhythm that would challenge the accuracy of the finest metronome. As the light grew dim, the images of the waves faded from view and Rachel relaxed in her recliner and drifted into a light sleep.

Suddenly, Rachel was pulled from her sleep as quickly as

a blacksmith draws hot steel from a fire to work and forge it into shape. At first, she didn't know what it was that woke her, but then she realized it was the overwhelming smell of vanilla.

Rachel turned to Gwen asking, "Do you smell that?"

"Smell what?" Gwen replied.

"The vanilla. It smells like an ice cream factory in here."

"I don't smell anything, honey. Are you feeling okay?"

"I'm fine. What do you mean, you don't smell anything?" Rachel replied, puzzled, sitting up straight in her chair.

"I'm telling you, Rachel, I don't smell anything. Maybe I'm just nose deaf."

"I smell vanilla in this house at least twice a month and you tell me you don't smell it?"

"No, honey, I don't. I guess that also explains why you're always asking me if I am baking something."

"I am going to find out where it's coming from, once and for all. I have never smelled it this strong before."

Rachel got up from her chair and took a deep breath, letting the smell grab her olfactory senses and drag her through the house. Like a dog in a cartoon, floating on the smell of cooking bacon, Rachel sniffed and whiffed her way through the house in search of the source of the sweet vanilla scent.

She walked toward the kitchen and the stairs that led upward. As she approached the bottom of the stairs on her way into the kitchen, a slight breeze blew past her carrying the overwhelming scent. A chill met her like an icy hand which made the hairs on her body stand up and caused goosebumps to rise on her battered and work-hardened skin. She felt as if a million ants were crawling all over her. There was nothing she could do to make the feeling subside.

Rachel began ascending the stairs; the first step groaned under her foot as if welcoming her to proceed. She cautiously walked up the remaining steps hearing only an occasional creak from the treads. At the top of the stairs, she began inspecting each of the rooms behind the three sturdy wooden doors. She opened each door carefully and stepped inside. She was startled when, at every door, the scent seemed to disappear as she entered. She stood brooding to herself, "How can this be?" The puzzle vexed her to her very soul.

Rachel returned to the landing at the top of the steps and again was assaulted by a vanilla-laden breeze. This time it was much stronger. With fierce determination, she peered up at the hatch leading to the attic. She considered the possibilities. *It can't be coming from there. The only things up there are boxes of old Christmas decorations and tax records.*

Rachel grabbed the short ladder that Gwen kept in one of the rooms and set it up under the hatch. She carefully climbed the rungs so as not to fall down the stairs to the first floor. She slowly opened the hatch and reached for the pull cord for the attic light. As she pulled the cord, the light burst to life, nearly blinding her with its powerful luminescence. At that very second, a much stronger wind blew past her from the opposite end of the attic. The air was musty and the smell of vanilla hung heavy in the air, nearly suffocating her as she fought to maintain her composure and balance. Her body tingled and she shook slightly in fear and anticipation; rare for a woman who feared so little.

She looked in the direction from which the wind blew. She knew there would be nothing there. After all, she had been in that attic hundreds of times and had never seen anything before. This time, though, things appeared to be different in the corner of the attic where the trusses met the wall. The light from the single bulb danced, casting odd shadows. Rachel could swear that in the shadows of the dim light she could see a dark shape, like a small box, barely peaking from behind the truss boards.

Rachel walked cautiously and deliberately across the ceiling joists making sure she did not fall through the old plaster ceiling below her. As she approached the corner, she could see that there was indeed a small wooden box in the corner. It appeared that the breeze blowing through the attic had dislodged the insulation, causing the box to become visible. She reached down and gently removed it from its hiding place, pulling the box to her bosom and holding it close as another strong breeze blew past her, taking the aroma of vanilla with it.

Everything became eerily silent and still, the hairs on her body standing on end. It was as if all the life had left the old house with the last breeze and the spirits could no longer speak to her. She made her way back to the hatch and down the way she had come.

Gwen sat in her chair knitting when Rachel returned to the den with her newly discovered prize. Rachel sat down in her chair and stared at the plain wooden box which wasn't much bigger than a shoebox. Gwen immediately stopped knitting and put her needles aside. She leaned forward in her chair and studied the old box with a look of curiosity and a bit of fear. "Where did you find that?" she asked.

"In the corner of the attic. It was hiding in the shadows under some insulation."

Gwen looked at her with an even greater look of curiosity. "That can't be. I've been all through that attic over the years and I had the insulation replaced about 15 years ago when we got rid of all the old asbestos in the house. It would have been discovered if it had been there."

"That's where I found it. What do you think's inside?"

"I couldn't tell you, honey." Gwen pulled up a small ottoman and sat down next to Rachel.

"Well, Grams, think we should open it?"

"Of course, silly! What good is a box if you don't open it and look inside?" Gwen replied with a slight giggle.

"It looks like we need a key," Rachel said, investigating the box closely. "Wait a minute, look at this."

"What is it? My eyes aren't as good as they used to be."

"It looks like a faint engraving. Maybe some scrollwork or fancy writing." Rachel carefully moved her hand over the irregular surface, her fingers tracing the intricate but worn engravings.

"Let's turn on some lights and I'll get my reading glasses."

"Grams, here are some initials in a fancy script. I think it reads 'W. A. K.' What do you think it means?"

"I'm not sure. I can't even muster a guess."

"Hey! Here's a date. It looks like… '1802.'"

"Wow, that's around the time this house was built. Wait a minute! I think this may have belonged to your great-great-great grandfather. At least I think that's enough 'Greats.'"

"What was his name?" Rachel asked.

"It's been a long time since I looked at our family tree, but I think it was William or something like that. Let me look in the family Bible. I'm sure he's listed there." Gwen picked up an old leather-bound Bible with an elegantly embossed cross on the surface. The edges were tattered and worn, pieces of the binding dried and broken; the black tanning worn through in areas revealing the brittle brown leather underneath. There were words on the cover that Rachel couldn't read, but she and Gwen knew them to read, "Hellige Bibel."

Gwen opened the book very slowly and carefully as fine particles of leather fell away from the binding under the strain. The old book rustled and crackled as if being woken from eternal sleep. Inside was an old piece of dingy paper that was nearly as fragile as the Bible itself. Gwen removed it and separated the folds as cautiously as she had opened the book. The paper sounded as if it was made of dried leaves rustling together. Once the paper was unfolded, Gwen began moving up the list of names, from the dark ones at the bottom which included Rachel's, to the older, faded names near the top. About halfway up, she found what she was looking for; there was a name, oddly darker than many of the others around it, the source of the mysterious initials on the box. "There he is," said Gwen, "one of your great-grandfathers, Wilhem Arvid Kristiansen."

"We know whose box it is now, so how do we open it? Should I get a screwdriver and pry it open?"

"This is a piece of family history nearly two hundred years old! Don't you dare! I keep a putty knife in the drawer in the kitchen." Gwen glanced at Rachel with a little smile and a twinkle in her eye.

Just then, Rachel had an epiphany and her expression turned to a look of excitement. "I know how to open it! I know where the key is! I'll get it!" Rachel shot out of her chair, nearly knocking Gwen over in the process. She stumbled frantically over the ottoman Gwen was sitting on as she lunged toward the fireplace and reached for the clock on the mantle. She opened the glass door covering the clock face; the hands were still locked in the same place they were the day her father died. She pulled the key from the winding mechanism and studied the head of the key. "See! Right here is the same fancy scrollwork and the same initials as the box! I knew I had seen that before!"

Gwen grabbed the key from Rachel's hand. "I never noticed those before, but then, I haven't touched that key since the day your dad died." A small tear gathered in the corner of her eye reflecting the flames of the fireplace. "Here, see if it fits."

Rachel took the key and placed it into the keyhole of the box. A perfect fit. She gently turned the key, being careful not to break the ancient lock. One click, two clicks, three clicks, and a loud clack as the latch unsettled from its rusty repose.

The lid of the box wiggled ajar ever so slightly, as if giving way to the bindings of age. With a groan like that of an old man getting up from a chair, the lock broke free and she flipped the lid back. Stopping its motion were small delicate leather straps to hold its weight.

Both women were startled and overcome with fear as the old clock on the shelf suddenly rang twice and began ticking away after so many years. A chill filled the room and both women trembled slightly in shock. Was this an omen from the Norse god Odin, a sign from God himself, or perhaps a message from a departed loved one who had been awoken from their eternal slumber? Or maybe it was just that the removal of the key itself had somehow released the internal mechanisms of the clockwork to allow it to move freely again and resume its operation. The women could only speculate its meaning or why after all this time it was this moment that the old clock decided to return to its appointed duty and record the minutes as they passed.

Chapter 7

SECRETS WITHIN

Inside the small chest, Gwen and Rachel could see three shriveled plants and another item that looked like a scroll. "Wow! Gramma, those look like vanilla beans." Rachel touched them gently and they disintegrated into a cloud of fine dust, releasing a final burst of vanilla essence into the air. Next, she picked up the small scroll and studied it carefully. She sniffed it, filling her lungs with the scent. "It's cinnamon! Could this be where those smells have been coming from all these years?"

"Could be, I suppose. What else is in there?"

"Nothing, nothing at all." Rachel cast a quizzical glance at Gwen.

"Wait a minute!" Gwen exclaimed. "Many families used to keep their valuables in these boxes when traveling, and many of them had hidden compartments."

Gwen reached for a tattered piece of ornate fabric in the bottom corner of the box that decorated the interior. She gave it a gentle tug and the bottom of the box rose slightly. She tugged a little harder and was able to place her finger under the edge of the bottom panel and lift it out of the way.

Both women huddled over the box like football players preparing for the final play of the big game. They peered into the hidden cavity in amazement; there, in the bottom of the box was a folded piece of stained linen with a bejeweled gold bracelet lying on top. Next to the parchment, lay a gold necklace chain. From it hung a beautiful pendant that appeared to have been cut from a reddish-colored geode. The geode slice had an odd shape with many crystalline facets adorning the edges of the center's opening. In one corner was a small piece of paper folded in quarters.

Rachel picked up the small piece of paper and opened it. The note was written in the most elegant script she had ever seen with loops and flourishes tracing every point of importance. She could not make out the writing as it appeared to be a strange code. Gwen peered at the paper and began to mumble quietly. "It's Norwegian!" Gwen blurted abruptly. "I'll translate it for you the best that I can, but some of the words seem a little odd to me. My Norwegian is also a little rusty…" She began to read slowly.

My Dearest Granddaughter,

I have prepared this chest of treasures that you might trace my steps and discover even greater rewards. I know you have found this, as I was told of this event by a voodoo priestess of whom I have made acquaintance during my travels and who has burdened me with visions that foreshadow my future. I know you are strong and of great knowledge. I know you are a child of the vast expanses of the treacherous deep. Take these items as my gift, and as a lamp to guide your way back to me. I await you in a place of enchantment and beauty. You need only to follow the sounds of the sea and songs of the Sirens. Take this map and these tokens, for they are the keys to the journey before you. Lose them not or all is lost. Seek me in the evening light in the dark shadows cast by a moon-filled sky, for here is where I dwell. What you seek is not of your world but of the distant past. Find me and treasures await you. Fail and a curse will vex you throughout your life. Through the waters of life, you must travel and in the darkness beneath them where Sirens, great creatures, and guardians take their leave, you will make a choice that will decide your fate. But fear not, for the sounds of the sea will guide you. Leave now, for only in the light of the full moon may your journey be fulfilled.

I wait for you in this place of damp recluse, that I may meet you and once again attain peace.

Forever and lovingly yours,

W.A.K.

Silence swept through the room where the two women stood, and a cold breeze overtook them. Goosebumps raised on their bodies as they shivered in shock and disbelief. Neither knew what to say or how to interpret the note.

Rachel spoke first. "Gramma, is this meant for you or me?"

Gwen raised her eyes slowly and looking deeply into her granddaughter's eyes, whispered softly, "Why, this is for you, honey. You are a child of the sea and a navigator of the waters. You have the spirit of an adventurer, and haven't you always had a feeling that something was tugging at you? Pulling you to a destiny greater than you know but have been unable to reach. This is your destiny. If these items are what I believe them to be, you have a great quest before you."

Rachel's face went pale and she could not speak. She glanced back into the box and picked up the bracelet and necklace.

Gwen smiled in a way Rachel had never seen before. Her smirk was slightly forced but wistfully happy. It dawned on

Rachel that it was a look of longing and sorrow. She knew that her grandmother wanted to travel on this journey and she also realized that it wasn't meant to be. But she was happy that Rachel was chosen to undertake this quest. "Put them on," Gwen said as she placed her hand around her granddaughter's shoulder and held out the necklace and bracelet.

Rachel carefully opened the hooked clasp on the necklace and attached it around her neck. It hung heavy between her breasts, under the weight of the large stone pendant.

"It's beautiful," said Gwen.

"Thanks, Grams."

Rachel slipped the bracelet over her hand and around her wrist. She then picked up the folded piece of linen parchment. It was heavy and smelled of cinnamon, vanilla, and an old attic. The edges along the folds were stained by time. She gently opened it.

Gwen realized immediately that it was a map, albeit an ancient one. Half sputtering, Gwen gasped at the map. "There isn't any writing on it. That could be anywhere. This could be a map of an area in the Mediterranean, the tropics, the North Atlantic, the South Pacific, anywhere!"

Rachel gazed at the map and pondered its meaning as it lay on the table. Rachel studied the contours of the landmasses. "You're right, this could be anywhere. There's no key, scale, or any identifiers. This could be a small bay or island on any body of water. How am I supposed to find this?!"

Gwen peered into the box where the map was tucked. "Maybe this is a clue; there are some long hairs, and something carved into the bottom of the box. It says, 'Beware Bonito.'"

"What do you think that means?"

"I haven't the foggiest idea, but I'm sure it's a clue to unlocking this puzzle," Gwen replied.

Gwen reached for a book from the shelf alongside the fireplace and began to page through it.

"What are you looking for?" asked Rachel.

"You know, honey, I haven't looked at this book in years; it's full of maritime folklore, stories about privateers and pirates and if I remember correctly, I read that name while paging through it a long time ago, but it was spelled 'B E N I T O.'"

At that moment, the front door flew open with a bang, startling Rachel and Gwen. Two women charged in. "Hey, Gramma! How's it hanging?" they yelled in unison. Gwen smiled widely as she dropped the book on the table and rushed toward the two figures.

"Low and to the left girls, low and to the left, and that's just the right tit. Don't have any idea where the left one's hanging." Gwen chuckled. She reached over and gave them each a strong hug and kiss. "I must say, Edith and Christin make a great couple, don't they, Rachel?"

"You know it, but you ought to hear them bitch at each other. Sounds like a couple of old seagulls fighting over a chicken bone."

"Well, we do love each other. Heck, I love Edith more than my brother, but then most of the time I'd like to kill my brother. What a jackass!" Christin bellowed out.

Edith said, "Yeah, and I love Christin almost as much as steak, pizza, and beer, in that order."

Edith and Christin leaned in and kissed each other gently on the lips. It was hard to tell who was more masculine. Both were quite attractive but after years working on a fishing boat, they both had the weathered look and muscled tone of a bodybuilder. No one wanted to tangle with either one of them in a bar brawl, but you always wanted them on your side as a friend. They had the looks of battered angels and the mouths of demonic sailors in spite of being well educated and having strong Christian upbringings. That is what life on the sea in a "man's world" will do to you. Adapt or be consumed and cast aside as weak and unfit.

Edith occasionally liked a pinch of chewing tobacco, but Christin preferred a stick of Big Red, and both were always chewing away with loud smacking sounds.

Christin yelled out with a look of disgust. "Edith! Get that shit out of your mouth next time you kiss me. Damn! It's like kissing a man and I ain't into that!"

Edith responded with a sly smirk. "Yes, dear, whatever you say."

"So, Grams, what are you two up to?" Christin inquired as she spanked the old woman firmly on her rear end.

"Looking over some old stuff we found in the attic."

"Really? Looks like someone is planning a trip to Panama."

Gwen was stunned. "What do you mean, Christin?"

"Look at that coastline there. See how it's shaped like the head of a dog? That's the southern part of Panama, where the canal comes through."

"Check out the map on the wall and see for sure. I'll be damned! It is Panama. Hey, Rachel, we know where you're going!" Gwen exclaimed.

"Panama? Haven't ever wanted to go there, but I guess we have to go now." Rachel laughed.

"What are you talking about?" Edith cautiously asked.

"Let's just say we've been given a challenge. We are being sent on a quest."

"A quest? And what do you mean *we*?"

"If I'm going to Panama, and I'm taking the boat, I sure as shit ain't flying. I'll need a crew," Rachel replied with a chuckle.

"Well, if *we* are going to Panama, *we* will need to know why, and what's in it for *us*?" said Christin sarcastically.

"I have a map and a mandate."

"A map of *what* and a mandate from *who*?"

"I don't quite know where the map leads us or where exactly we are going," Rachel replied, "but the mandate comes from my great-great-great-grandfather."

"You gotta be shittin' me?" Edith said.

"Nope, you both in?"

"Sure, if the pay's right," said Christin.

"You bet, but we need to know what we're going there for; especially if this isn't going to be a vacation," Edith followed.

"I wish I knew," said Rachel. "All I do know is that I need to go someplace on this map in search of my grandfather who has a connection to someone or something named Bonito."

"Oh yeah, I need to finish looking that up," added Gwen. "Let me grab that book again. Well, look at that, it opened to the page I was searching for. Here is a section on Benito Bonito, who was also known as 'Bloody Sword Bonito,' a pirate."

"A pirate!" replied Christin.

"Yes, a pirate. Here is what it says," began Gwen.

Chapter 8

THE LEGEND OF BENITO "BLOODY SWORD" BONITO

Benito Bonito was known by the name, Bennett Graham, before becoming a pirate. He was thought to have served as an officer in the Royal Navy and believed that he had possibly served directly under Admiral Nelson.

After his service, it was believed that Bennett took the name Benito Bonito to aid in hiding his true identity, and through his ruthless actions, he was given the moniker "Bloody Sword." Some speculate that his reign of terror began in the Caribbean where he began collecting his famous treasure. To escape capture, some claim that he sailed south and rounded Cape Horn, resulting in his operations moving to the west coast of the Americas; a very daring move in those tumultuous times.

According to some accounts, Benito began his west coast conquests around 1818, on his ship the *Relampago*, which he had captured during a battle that saw his own ship destroyed. With his new ship, he spent much of his time looting and burning Spanish galleons and hoarding whatever treasures he managed to steal.

In one of his more famous attacks, he discovered that a large amount of Spanish gold was to be moved from the Mexican cordillera to Acapulco. Benito hatched a daring plan involving his own crew. Once all the details of the move became known, Benito had several members of his crew capture the guards who were sent to escort the gold. His men then dressed in the guards' uniforms and proceeded to escort and load the gold onto Benito's ship without incident. Benito sailed away with the treasure without having fired a single shot.

Benito is thought to have hidden his pirated treasures somewhere on Cocos Island about 300 miles off the coast of Costa Rica. Some say it was buried in the sand of Wafer Bay, while others say it was placed in a cave and sealed for eternity.

During his brief rule of the high seas, Benito battled many warships that were sent to end his reign of terror. It's believed that Benito's bold offensive assaults on warships throughout his career went well until he was finally defeated at the Bay of Buena Ventura. Benito was taken to England, tried and hanged, thus, taking his secrets and the location of his plundered treasures with him.

The story of Benito Bonito is complex and difficult to verify. This entry is merely a single account of many that have been passed down through the years. Most accounts were verbally passed around trading ports and due to miscommunication and embellishment; the stories of this vicious pirate have become tainted with legend, lies, facts, and lore. Because there is little recorded history of these accounts, it is difficult to validate many of the ideas presented here and little credence can be given to their accuracy.

What is known is that a man named Bennett Graham did exist. There are legendary accounts of a pirate by the name of

Benito Bonito and many believe that whatever hoard he had accumulated was buried and/or hidden on Isla del Coco off the coast of Costa Rica. Should anyone attempt to search for such a treasure, we wish you well in your pursuits. It is said that the treasure is protected by guardians living in the depths of the sea as well as an ancient curse. Legend also states that no man will ever recover the riches of Benito Bonito.

Chapter 9

WHERE DO WE GO FROM HERE?

After Gwen had finished reading the chapter, Rachel said, "Okay, so we know that we are probably looking at this little island here on the map. Since we know this is Panama and Benito sailed west, this must be Cocos Island. We can only assume there is a connection between my grandfather and this pirate."

Edith shifted her weight and glanced down at a piece of wood near her foot. "So what does this mean?" she asked as she picked up the panel and studied its back.

"It's just the panel that covered a secret compartment in the bottom of the chest on the table," Rachel replied.

"Yeah, but it has writing on the back."

"Writing? Show me!" Gwen blurted abruptly. Once in her shaking hands, she studied the writing intently. "There is another message written on the back in Norwegian; I'll try to translate it."

The treasure you seek can only be found by the secrets

contained in your heart. The path you seek is revealed only by following the light of the moon.

Seek me. I await.

W.A.K. Quartermaster—Relampago

"You gotta be shittin' me!" Rachel exclaimed. "You mean good ole Granddad was a freakin' pirate. Ain't that a boot to the crotch? And to think, he was a mate to 'Bloody Sword,' so he may have actually known where some of this treasure was buried." Whenever the girls were around, Rachel's vocabulary became much more flowery.

Christin turned toward Rachel. "I know what you're thinking. When do we leave?"

Edith interjected. "Wait a minute, now. We may know where we're going, but we don't know what we're looking for or even where to look."

Rachel had a smirk on her face. The others could tell she was working things out in her head. "We'll just figure it out as we go. It's a long trip and we will have plenty of time along the way."

Edith said, "So that's your whole plan?! You're gonna treat this like a fishing trip and just point the bow out to sea, sniff the wind, and go for it until your gut tells you where to drop the nets? We're just going to take the boat, sail to some island in the Pacific in search of some legendary treasure that may not even exist, that no man is meant to ever discover. Not to mention, we don't know where to look! We have a map with nothing on it and a letter written by a seemingly half-crazy pirate's mate. Am I reading you right here?"

Rachel quipped, "Yep, that's about it. It's worked up to this point, hasn't it? And by the way, we aren't men."

"Okay, the major fishing seasons are over for a few months,

I got nothing better to do than get drunk and screw Christin 'til she's sore. What the hell, let's go."

"When can you two have the boat ready, if I get the money out of the bank and get the provisions ordered?"

Christin and Edith looked at each other and replied in unison, "Three days," which was their standard answer for such inquiries.

"We'll leave Sunday morning after the sunrise church service. I want to be sure that if we are doing this, we get one last blessing before heading out. You guys get the boat ready, and I'll get the charts and make our arrangements for the canal crossing. I'll even pick up a Spanish to English dictionary."

"Damn, Rachel," Edith replied. "Wouldn't want you to strain yourself or anything. You want me to come with you to carry that dictionary, so you don't sprain your wrist or break a nail?"

"I am the captain and owner of the boat. You want a piece of the loot; you'll do as you're told."

Christin chimed in. "Geez, you really can be a bitch. It's a good thing we love ya and promised Gwen a long time ago that we wouldn't kill you unless we had to."

"I appreciate it, girls. I'll see you both soon then. Standard procedures until we depart. Now let's get on the stick."

"Thanks for keeping that promise, girls," Gwen said. "I know how hard it must be some days, but I don't know what I would do without Rachel. Of course, I don't know what I would do without any of you. I love you all. You are all my family."

"We love you, too, Gramma Gwen. You feed us, treat us like family, and don't judge us. Hell, you could probably beat us up, ya tough old broad."

"You girls want to spend the night here and get an early

start in the morning?" Gwen inquired as she turned to go into the kitchen.

"We will if you can stand all the banging and groaning sounds." Rachel knew that the girls hadn't had a chance to be together in weeks since the season began. "Heck, we would be in bed right now if we didn't have to get something to eat before we wasted away."

"So long as part of the 'banging' is the sounds of pots and pans in the morning when you make me breakfast, I don't care if you drive Christin's head through the wall. By the way, I like my coffee black, just like the edges around my pancakes." Gwen smiled.

"You got it, Grams." Edith snapped a rather impressive military salute, bringing the heels of her boots together with a sharp click.

"Well, it's 11:30. I'm tired and it has been quite an evening, so I'm going to bed. I'll see you all in the morning. I love you." Gwen made the rounds, hugging each of the girls and kissing them gently on the cheek.

Rachel and the girls followed shortly behind.

Rachel lay in her bed that night and stared at the ceiling in the dim glow of her alarm clock. She thought about the morning and what lay ahead. Numerous possibilities and scenarios swirled through her mind until she finally drifted into a restless sleep filled with visions of what may lay ahead and the dread of the unknown.

Chapter 10

DEPARTING IS SUCH SWEET SORROW

The sun rose slowly Sunday morning, dancing along the horizon and gently peeking over the edge before revealing itself in full glory. Edith and Christin were loading the last of the provisions and doing the final equipment checks prior to departing, while Rachel reviewed the weather forecast. She was concerned about a depression making its way toward them; they would have to leave soon if they had any chance of missing the worst of it. They had been through worse, but this time they were going to be closer to shore and in shallower waters where the effects of the waves, winds, and currents would be heightened.

Rachel reached for the marine radio mic. "Harbormaster, *Lady Destiny*, inquiring as to the status of float plan filed and approval for departure." *Lady Destiny II* was the boat's real name since the first one belonged to Rachel's father. Most of the time, she dropped the second generation suffix out of convenience.

"*Destiny*, Harbormaster. Coast Guard has approved float plan and departure. Heavy traffic at last marker buoy, departure window set for zero seven hundred hours until zero eight hundred hours."

"Roger, Harbormaster. *Destiny* out."

Rachel slid the cabin window open and yelled down to Edith and Christin, who had just arrived on deck from their engineering checks. "Hey, ladies! You ready? We got a thirty-minute window to beat the weather."

Edith responded with her shrill yell, "Give us ten minutes to grab an extra fifteen gallons of lube oil! We got a small leak in the auxiliary pump and if we're required to use it, we want to be sure we have enough oil to make it to a port! I'm just gonna run up to the supply shack and get it!"

"Okay! Make it quick, we gotta make waves, soon!"

Rachel settled back into her chair. Her demeanor changed at sea and she became much more in tune with her surroundings as well as taking on a more coarse and unrefined personality to match that of her feisty crew. She never felt more at home than when she was sitting in her captain's chair. It cradled and surrounded her like an old friend with the gentle touch of an impassioned lover. With her boat and her chair, she didn't need anyone else, and she was fine with that. No drama, no complications, no fighting, only the deep drone of the two big diesels under her feet that hummed a familiar and comforting tune.

There was a sudden knock at the cabin door and it immediately slid open. In the doorway stood a tall man with weathered features, a neatly trimmed beard, and long salt and pepper hair. The bags under his eyes reflected the hard life of a fisherman and how the hours wore on the human body. He had a broad smile surrounded by his large, bushy beard which trapped small bits of tobacco and smelled of coffee, with a cigarette dangling from his chapped lips.

"Permission to come aboard?" growled the weathered figure.

"Permission granted! Pete, you old dog. What brings you this way?"

"I heard the engines come to life and I know you don't fish this season, so I was wondering what was going on."

"Me and the girls are gonna take the *Lady* out for a couple weeks and head down south for some time away. It's been a good year and they deserve it."

"With this front coming in, don't you think it would be better to wait a couple of days?"

"We've been through worse, just like you. We aren't too worried, and we have a good departure time, so we should be able to beat the worst of it."

"Either way, you need to be careful. I've lost too many friends because they thought they could beat the weather, but the old sea, she doesn't care if you are God-fearing, stout-hearted, young, old, wise or foolish. She will chew you up and spit you out if you're not careful."

"Pete, we have all lost loved ones to the sea, and I don't take chances without calculating the risks first. I would appreciate a blessing from ya if you don't mind?"

Pete was once an ordained Methodist minister before finding out there was more money in fishing. Plus, he had the freedom to cuss at will. The two bowed their heads as Pete began, "Sure thing… we pray that the glory of God be around you and watch over you. That He grant you fair winds and following seas, and that He keep you in His graces until you safely return to walk among us again. AMEN."

"AMEN!"

"Thanks. You know that means a lot to me. You've been like a father, a brother, an uncle, and a tough boss to me. I owe you so much." Pete had taught and guided her through the years after her father passed. "Thank you. Keep a weather eye out and I'll look you up as soon as we get back to port."

"You do that, Rachel." Pete leaned in and gave her a peck on the cheek and then turned to leave. Rachel reached over and grabbed him by the arm pulling him in close. She didn't normally show weakness or affection, but this time she hugged Pete with all the strength in her body. She broke the embrace with a quiet whisper in Pete's ear, "I love you, old man. I don't tell you enough." Pete returned her affection with a broad smile and a wink as he again turned to depart the cabin.

"Oh, Pete?" Rachel asked abruptly. "Will you look in on Gwen while we're gone?"

"I'll be glad to. You be safe now and get outta here before you get stuck in port."

"Will do. See you soon."

"Bye now, baby girl."

"See ya, Big Daddy."

Pete slid the door shut and stepped off the boat just as Edith and Christin loaded the last of the buckets of oil onboard.

Rachel slid the window open once more, and called to the girls, "Hey, you two broads ready to kick this mule?"

"Aye, aye, Captain!" they replied in unison and offered a half-hearted Benny Hill salute followed by a middle finger, which was customary for this crew when casting off.

Pete just shook his head and continued walking down the pier with a smile on his tattered face. "You girls take it easy and have a good trip. Take care of each other and I'll pray for you every day," he shouted.

Christin and Edith looked up for a moment and waved at Pete with excited smiles. "See you soon, Big Daddy!" This crew had always called Pete "Big Daddy" ever since they left the service of his command aboard his fishing trawler on summer breaks from school.

Edith tended the fore line, Christin the aft; in less than a minute they were pulling away from the pier.

"Harbormaster, *Lady Destiny*, making turns and proceeding to buoys."

"Roger that, *Destiny*; good luck. Float plan is now in force at zero-seven-three-eight. Be advised of two large container ships in your lanes, 15 miles."

"Roger, Harbormaster."

They proceeded slowly through the harbor to keep their wake to a minimum, so as to not raise the ire of the harbor patrol or the harbormaster, who was undoubtedly watching their every move. Even though they had made this trek hundreds of times, the harbormaster was from another time. He still believed that women did not belong on boats and sure as hell shouldn't be captains. He was always looking for some way to come down on them and make things harder than they needed to be. Yet, deep inside everyone knew he cared more for this rag-tag crew than all the others and saw himself as their ever watchful, albeit crotchety, protector.

Lady Destiny made her way past the first set of buoys, then the second, to finally reach the third and last set. They were now in open water where they were free to do as they pleased. Rachel picked up the mic. "Gloucester Harbor, *Lady Destiny*, cleared final marker and proceeding with float plan."

There was a brief pause that seemed longer than normal, then the radio cracked to life. An old familiar voice boomed over the speaker, "Roger, *Destiny*. Continue per plan."

Rachel reached over and opened the throttles of the two big diesels, awakening them from a mild purr into a full-on roar, like two mighty lions waking from their slumber. She switched the mic over to the intercom and reported down to the girls on deck. "Okay, ladies, we are on our way. Let's do another full set of checks on the systems, clean the crap out of the seawater strainers, and make sure all our hatches are dogged.

I'll take the first watch and you guys can make lunch. We still have work to do."

From below, Christin grabbed the intercom knob, and with a snarky response, proclaimed, "No shit! We're already on it. Not like we haven't done this before."

Rachel smiled and eased back into her chair. In the distance, she could see the first of the two container ships bearing down on her. She made a course adjustment to move out of its direct path and gave a wide berth to keep from being capsized by the ship's mighty wake when it passed.

The engines droned a familiar song that quickly lulled Rachel into her comfort zone. Instinctively, she checked her GPS programming and maps once more to verify their route.

The *Lady Destiny* finished its turn to the south just as the container ship passed by them. There was a good half-mile between the two ships, but it didn't seem to be nearly enough considering their size difference, especially when the three main waves created by the container ship's wake hit their tiny trawler. Rachel radioed down over the intercom, "Three big ones coming in, be ready for the first one in ten." Ten seconds later, the first wave overtook them and tossed their tiny craft around like a fishing bobber. Bangs, clanks, and crashes could be heard all over the ship. Rachel knew immediately that one of the galley doors wasn't properly secured, and all the dishes fell out on the deck. The next two waves passed with little consequence.

A minute later Edith poked her head into the cabin with one hand securing a bloody towel to her scalp and called up, "Hey, Rach, think you could give us a little more notice next time? I damn near killed myself on a valve down here." Edith never called Rachel, 'Rach,' unless in jest or if she was really pissed off. Rachel knew immediately that it wasn't in jest.

"Sorry, I didn't think they would be that bad and they were so smooth that they were hard to judge in this calm sea."

Edith went back to the engine room and finished her tasks quickly. She then proceeded to the galley, where Christin was already picking up the fallen dishes and working on lunch.

Christin glanced at Edith and did a double take. "Damn, girl, next time hit back. Let me look at that gash." She peeled the towel back from Edith's head as thick red blood flowed from the wound and through her dark black hair. "Oh! Ouch! That doesn't look too good. I'm gonna have to put a couple stitches in there."

"No way! I hate the way you stitch. Just get the superglue and glue it up. I'll be careful and not tear it open 'til it heals."

"Okay, but it's awfully big."

"I don't care, just do it and hand me some Ibuprofen. I have one hell of a headache."

Christin cleaned the wound and poured in a generous amount of hydrogen peroxide as Edith began uncontrollably cursing. She was able to glue the wound shut once the foaming of the peroxide stopped and attempted to cover it with a bandage which was made more difficult by Edith's thick black hair. Edith slammed four Ibuprofen and lay down on the galley bench. She drifted off for a short nap while Christin finished cooking.

Chapter 11

GIRLS WILL BE GIRLS

Up to this point, the trip had been relatively uneventful. They made it out of Gloucester just in time to miss the major weather. The watch rotations became regular as clockwork and a lull fell over the boat.

After nearly half a week of slowly churning down the Atlantic coast with the constant twinkle of lights dancing off the starboard side of the boat every night, everyone was becoming weary of the monotony. With nothing to do, this trip was turning out to be tougher than hauling nets. The hotter daytime temperatures were also becoming unbearable, especially for a crew that was accustomed to the much cooler temperatures of Maine and the Grand Banks near Newfoundland.

Rachel eased the boat into a slip in the Key West marina with hardly a nudge against the mooring bumpers. Edith and Christin carefully tied up the rusty and weathered trawler, as many locals and tourists looked on with disgust or curiosity. In a marina full of multimillion-dollar yachts and exotic speed boats, a northern fishing trawler was an unusual and most unwelcome sight.

One yacht owner, moored a couple of slips away, came down as the two bikini-clad crew members finished hooking up the shore power lines and freshwater connections. "Hello, ladies," he said in an effeminate voice. With a smirk, he inquired, "Do you really think this is the proper place to dock this type of vessel? Seems to me you would be better off over at the fishing docks, down the way."

Edith glanced over her shoulder at the man who was sipping a hurricane in the balmy Florida heat. She turned around, grabbed the drink from his hand, pulled out the straw and chugged the rest of the drink in front of him as he stood in silent and motionless disbelief. She winked at him as she handed the empty glass back. "Ah! I needed that. It's so hot down here, I feel like I have a squid living in between my ass cheeks."

The man flushed with anger. "Around here, we're a bit more sophisticated and we don't act like common, uneducated riff-raff."

Edith knew she was getting the best of him. "Well, I may be riff-raff, but I also have a master's in maritime engineering from the Marine Maritime Academy in Castine, Maine, so I would check the attitude, old man. And by the way, we aren't here working. We're here visiting and this was one of the only berths big enough for this beast, so unless you want me to shove my foot up your ass, you should waddle back to your floating double-wide mobile home and let us enjoy ourselves."

"This conduct is unacceptable! I will have the harbormaster eject you immediately!"

"If you do that, old man, I will hunt you down and when I find you, I'll hang you from the radio mast by the short hairs on your ass and feed you chum. If you've got the balls, try me!

I'm more of a man than you'll ever be. Now run along and take a shower. You reek of fear or urine. I can't tell which."

The man turned away, his face crimson with rage as he pounded up the dock to the harbormaster's office.

About ten minutes later, a neatly dressed man in his fifties approached the *Lady Destiny* as Edith and Christin were sunbathing on the aft deck in a couple of lawn chairs and waiting for Rachel to join them.

He removed his hat, placing it across his chest, exposing his perfectly trimmed salt and pepper hair. He cleared his throat and announced, "Hello, ladies. I'm the harbormaster, Captain Dumfries."

Christin tilted her head up and lifted her sunglasses. "Hey, Captain. What can we do you for?"

"I got a complaint from one of our locals that there was some activity on this vessel that was not conducive to an environment of camaraderie."

"So, you mean the old man squealed like a pig about us docking here."

"In a manner of speaking, yes. I have never seen Mr. Miles so bent out of shape. I have assured him that you are properly docked and in compliance with the marina's rules."

"So, what's the problem?" Edith inquired.

Captain Dumfries looked down with a slight grin as he returned his cap to his head and smoothed his white, immaculately tailored uniform with his hand. "Old man Miles has been a thorn in my side for years. I just wanted to thank you for finally putting him in his place. I also wanted to let you know that you and this beautiful old rust bucket are welcome here. If you need anything, just let me or my staff know."

At that moment Rachel emerged from the cabin after overhearing the conversation. "How about dinner?"

Puzzled, Captain Dumfries responded, "Excuse me, but what do you mean?"

"Simple," Rachel quipped. "We just got into port, we need to refuel and re-provision, and we are all hungry as hell. How 'bout you show us around since we don't know the area, and we'll take you out to dinner?"

"As harbormaster, I am not inclined to show favoritism, so I must decline your offer. However, if you happened to stop by Sloppy Joe's on Duval Street after 8:00 p.m., there is a good chance you might run into someone you know."

"Great! It's a date." Rachel settled into her lounge chair and slid her sunglasses down over her eyes. "Anything else?"

"No, that'll do for now. Have a good day, ladies."

Christin yelled back, "Catch ya' later, Cap!" Captain Dumfries gave a quick salute to the women and returned to his duties.

Edith and Christin looked over at Rachel, who was relaxing in her orange bikini with her pasty white skin glowing in the Florida sun. Edith was the first to comment. "Damn, girl, we've never seen you in anything less than jeans and a flannel shirt. You have one kick-ass body!" Rachel didn't know how to respond, and she did something she'd never done before. For just a moment she blushed.

"I bought this bikini special for the trip."

Christin chimed in. "Well, that's a smokin' hot bikini; and if you ever want to consider a three-way, just let me know."

"Stop it! You know I'm not that way, but I must say, I've never seen you guys looking so good, either. Enjoy your time here; when this is over it'll be back home and back to the cold."

Christin began slathering sunscreen on Rachel before she had a chance to realize what was happening. Rachel let her finish since, with her fair skin, she knew she would need it; and it gave Christin a cheap thrill. For a moment, Rachel just enjoyed the touch of another human, something she hadn't felt in many years.

The three settled into their chairs for a long, lazy afternoon, lying under the sun and drinking in the joy of pure relaxation. Edith repositioned her ballcap down over her eyes to relieve pressure from the still-tender bruise she was nursing. She cranked the volume of her headphones, her head bobbing in time with Van Halen's "Panama."

That evening, the three dressed in shorts, tank tops, and flip flops, and walked into town heading down Duval Street to Sloppy Joe's. They quickly made their way to the bar, where they found Captain Dumfries nursing a rum and Coke.

"Hey, Cap!" Rachel exclaimed.

"I'm off duty, so please call me John."

"Okay, John. I'm Rachel, Captain of the *Lady Destiny II*, and these are my crew—Edith and her partner Christin."

John glanced over and immediately became transfixed on Christin. Under the neon glow of the bar lights, he could see the outline of her braless size D's through her tank top.

Edith smiled and chuckled a bit. "Yeah, aren't they great? They're all mine," she said as she grabbed a good handful.

Christin swatted her away. "You can't do that here!"

John chuckled. "Girls, just about anything goes here. Hell, body paint is considered proper attire on Duval Street. Sorry for staring."

"No harm done. I'm just yanking your chain," Edith said with a smile. "So, what do they have to eat in this place?"

"Let's get a table and I'll take care of ordering for you."

"Why, thank you, John." Rachel said as she passed him a sly wink.

At the table, John ordered a selection of appetizers: conch fritters, arepas, and conch chowder, followed by the main course of the Sloppy Joe specialty, South Carolina pulled pork sandwiches, and mojo pork tacos. He followed up the meal with "the must-have" when in Key West: four fresh slices of Key lime pie.

They laughed and talked till the wee hours of the morning. Each of them indulged in several cocktails of their choice. John and Rachel stuck to rum and Cokes; Edith drank scotch and soda; and, Christin consumed copious amounts of frozen margaritas. When all was said and done, they were all very unsteady and walking proved quite a feat.

As they staggered out of the bar, John said, "Since none of us are doing too good right now, how 'bout we go back to my place and crash? It's only a couple blocks and I have plenty of room."

The three women, almost in unison, replied, "Sure, why not."

The next morning, the sun blazed through the slits in the blinds and assaulted Christin's face. She tried to open her eyes, but it felt like someone had poured half the beach in them. Her eyes burned and itched and that didn't even begin to describe the pain in her head. It thumped in time with her own heartbeat. "Oh shit, I haven't felt this bad since I had pneumonia a couple of years back. Hey, Edith, get up."

Edith covered her head with a pillow and in muffled tones, Christin heard her say, "Fuck off, bitch."

"Oh, come on, you can sleep later. We need to go and check on the boat. Where's Rachel?"

Again, in muffled tones, "How the hell should I know? Go find her."

Christin straightened herself out as much as possible and pulled her long red hair back in a ponytail, then began to traipse through the small home. She checked every room until she happened upon the last closed door at the end of the hallway. Carefully, she cracked it open and peeked inside. There, on the bed, she could see Rachel's naked sleeping body entwined with John's. She drank in the sight for several seconds, and then she quietly closed and re-latched the door and slipped back down the hall. She found Edith standing in the middle of the kitchen with a cup of coffee. She went over to plant a kiss on her lips.

"Nice, what was that for?"

"I just want you to know I love you. Can I have a sip?"

"Sure, where's Rachel?"

"She'll be along later. We'll head back to the boat and she'll be there in a little while."

Edith and Christin found a bottle of Tylenol above the kitchen sink and they both swallowed a hefty handful.

"Okay, let's go," Edith said, as she pinched Christin firmly on her right butt cheek.

They exited the house, gained their bearings with the assistance of a small tourist map they'd picked up the night before. They traced out the route and in no time they had made their way back to the boat.

Once back at the boat, the girls slogged their way wearily through their chores and prepared to depart.

Several hours later as they lay on the deck sunning themselves, they could see two figures walking down the dock holding hands. Rachel's pink, sunburned complexion shone in stark contrast to that of the well-tanned figure at her arm. Rachel and John stopped at the edge of the boat and held an embrace while they shared a long kiss.

Rachel looked at John with warm eyes. "Thank you for a wonderful evening. I wish we weren't leaving so soon but we have a tight schedule to keep."

"That's okay. You know where to find me on your way back through."

"Sure, I'll see you around, Cap." She kissed him one more time on the lips and turned to her boat. He held her hand as she boarded across the gangway until the very last second, then finally, he turned away so they wouldn't have to say goodbye.

"So, did he teach you how to mambo last night?" Edith quipped.

"I had a wonderful time. I haven't felt this close to anyone since my father died, and I think it was the same for him. His wife died two years ago, and he has immersed himself in work. It was nice." Rachel knew it wasn't meant to be, but for a few fleeting hours, they found solace in each other.

"I'm proud of you, girl. You hide your pain and loneliness, but Christin and I know you too well. You needed last night more than anyone and I can see it in your bloodshot eyes."

"Alright, don't you have work to do?"

"All done, Captain, just awaiting your orders."

"Then get your butt up and let's get this girl turnin' and churnin'. We gotta be in Cancun in a couple of days."

"Aye, aye, Captain." And with her hand cupped around her mouth like a megaphone, Edith yelled, "Hey, Christin! The bitch is back! We gotta go."

From below, they could hear Christin shout, "Glad to hear it. Let's float this boat. I'm tired of racing the buoys and I've never seen Cancun. Put the screws to it!"

Chapter 12

TEMPEST SONGS

They were little more than half a day out of Cancun, just south of the Yucatan Peninsula, and things were looking bad. She had been tracking an ominous-looking front since they'd left port in Key West and she knew they would hit it head-on. They didn't have time to wait it out, so Rachel pushed the *Lady Destiny* forward into the belly of the beast. High seas and a dangerous squall line meant that they wouldn't be sleeping any time soon.

Dawn broke with Rachel manning the wheelhouse in a fight to save her crew and ship. They had been through many rough seas before and this was comparable to some of the storms they had experienced while fishing off the Grand Banks. Although they had been through similar storms, this one, somehow, felt different. Rachel was genuinely worried and uneasy.

She wasn't sure if it was just because the waters were warmer, making the wind and waves slightly different, but this storm felt as if it was coming directly at them. Every wave and gust of wind tried to impede their progress and prevent them from succeeding in their quest. The ship creaked and shuttered as wave after wave pounded the thick steel hull, and the *Lady Destiny* groaned, as if in agony from the forces trying to break her will and tear her apart.

Edith and Christin were down below trying to manage the engine room and keep everything running. Edith popped her head into the access way that led from the lower decks to the wheelhouse. "Hey, Rachel, I know you're doing your best, but we gotta be careful or all hell is going to break loose down here."

"I know! I know!" Rachel shouted back. "Without the nets and without any cargo in the holds, we're riding higher than normal. I'm doing everything I can to keep us from capsizing."

"We gotta do something to keep the seawater inlets submerged and keep the screws in the water. Every time the screws come out, the engines race and if it goes on much longer, we're going to blow one or both of the turbos up. When the seawater inlets are uncovered, we suck air through the pumps, causing us to lose prime and cooling. The last thing we need out here is a runaway diesel. The turbos are glowing yellow hot as it is," Edith spat.

"If you can do any better, then do it. Right now, I have an idea and I need your help. Come up here and help me activate the pumps and charge seawater into the cargo wells to give us some ballast to trim this thing out."

"That's a good idea, I'm on it, but I gotta get down below and help Christin. She thinks we're about to lose one of the seawater pumps. We have both mains and the auxiliary running, plus, we have the bypass open to try and maximize flow and cooling, but it doesn't help much if we're suckin' air in these warm waters."

"No, shit! That's why we need to get our belly lower. These waves are big and they're trying to tear us to pieces. Every time they hit it feels like they're coming straight through the windows at me. I can barely hold us in a position to intercept them. She wants to turn sideways like an old mule and if she succeeds, we are all done for."

"Okay, Rachel, I've got the pumps flooding the bays. I hope it helps."

"It has to."

"I'm going down below for a minute. I'll be back up in a few to check the cargo holds to see how they are filling." Edith disappeared down the narrow ladder and back to the engine room to check on Christin. She found her standing between the engines doing her best to stay upright and keep an eagle eye on the seawater pumps that brought the vital cooling water into the ship. That water was the lifeblood of the engines and other systems. Without cooling water, it didn't matter how much fuel they had, the engines and compressors would seize, and they would be dead in the water at the mercy of the torrent outside.

Edith looked through the deck plates under her feet and saw the bilges taking on water. "Hey, Christin?! Where's all this water coming from?" she shouted.

"I'm not sure. I just switched on the auxiliary bilge pump to help the main keep up until we pin it down. I thought it was one of the seawater pumps or an isolation valve, but I can't find it."

The noise in the engine room was deafening and both women were having trouble hearing each other. Edith worked her way through the narrow space around Christin and headed further aft. She had a hunch but hoped she was wrong. She turned on a battery-powered emergency lantern and pointed it toward the most distant recesses of the ship. There, in the beam of the lantern light, her fears were confirmed.

"Christin! We are in deep shit here, come help me."

"What?!" Christin replied with a loud yell.

Edith grabbed Christin by the arm and yanked her from her perch to point out the toolbox strapped to the deck.

"Okay, I'll bring it," she managed to blurt out before grabbing it.

Edith began working her body through the narrow openings between the pipes and equipment to gain access to the bowels of the ship. She finally arrived at the aft-most point of the ship where the shaft penetrated the hull and transferred the energy of the engines and reduction gears to the large bronze screws on the other side of the bulkhead. She saw seawater pouring into the boat from around one of the propeller shafts.

"Christin, the shaft seals are failing from all the pounding and over-speeding of the shaft! I'm going to open up the shaft seal oil supply to try and slow this down while I tighten the primary packing down! Give me that big crescent wrench!"

Christin handed Edith the wrench just as she finished opening the shaft lube oil valve. Edith immediately began tightening the dozen or so large nuts that held the shaft packing assembly in place to try and slow down the leak. She saw that her efforts were not in vain as the flow of water began to subside. But she wondered to herself, *Will it be enough for the pumps to keep up?* The water had slowed from a constant stream to a fine spray that stung Edith's face and blinded her. She yelled to Christin once more, "Give me the secondary seal material and retaining ring parts!"

Christin jockeyed herself into a better position and opened an aluminum box containing the spare parts. She handed Edith the packing materials. After being assembled, the parts formed a ring with holes that matched the same pattern as the studs that secured the main shaft seal assembly. Edith knew this would be dangerous. Trying to install the packing material around the shaft and then placing the retaining ring in place while the shaft was still turning was probably the most dangerous thing you could do. She turned toward Christin, who instinctively handed her a grease gun and a paintbrush.

Edith saturated the shaft with grease and then added the packing material in hopes that it would be slick enough to prevent the packing from getting wound up on the shaft, pulling her to her death. She began working the packing material into the narrow opening around the shaft with a putty knife, a punch, and a hammer. Once she had worked a few wraps into the opening and around the shaft, she placed the seal plate over the studs that protruded from the seal assembly. Christin handed her the extra nuts and Edith made short work of installing them while struggling to keep from being pulled into the rotating shaft whirling before her. She snugged the nuts against the plate, being careful to make sure the tension was equal across the whole assembly. The water slowed to a small trickle, which was perfect since it helped to lubricate the new seal material and prevent it from burning up from friction.

Emerging from the dark recesses of the engine room, Edith stretched. She was hot, wet, and covered with grease. Her face was sweaty and her eyes burned from the saltwater. Her left forearm was bloodied and raw from where it had rubbed against the rotating shaft as she was tightening the nuts. The shaft had peeled the skin away just like when she was a child and fell off her bike and skidded across the pavement on her knees. This pain was compounded by the constant intrusion of saltwater into the wound from her drenched clothing.

Christin pointed to the wound. "You're hurt!"

"It's just a rug burn. Hell, you've given me worse on a Saturday night."

The two sat bow-legged on the deck plates near the seawater pumps. Edith noted, "Those pumps aren't as hot as they were."

"Nope. Seems that they're getting more water now and less air."

Edith jumped up. "Oh shit! I gotta stop the other pumps before we flood!" She ran toward the ladder at the front of the compartment and headed up to the wheelhouse. She reached the pump control panel and switched off the pumps that were filling the cargo holds. The holds were just about two-thirds full, which added just enough ballast to make the ship more manageable in the turbulent seas.

"I didn't think you were ever coming back!" Rachel proclaimed.

"I was busy saving our asses and I had to take an engineer's shower back at the shaft seals."

"I see that. Looks like you could use another one."

"Yeah, maybe when this weather breaks a bit." Edith wiped her hands and face on a rag that was lying on the pump control panel. "I'm going below to see what else I can do."

As Edith turned to descend the ladder, an alarm pierced the roar of the tempest outside. Edith shuddered at the alarm panel and saw that the auxiliary seawater pump indicator was lit up. She silenced the alarm and raced back to the engine room.

Christin was surrounded by a blue-gray fog and the place reeked of burnt varnish and plastic. She had just turned off the breaker to the pump and was coughing on the fumes. "It's only the auxiliary so we're okay, but we need to close the isolation valves, so we don't get any more leaks," Christin shouted, as she wiped tears from her eyes caused by the burning fumes.

Edith closed one valve as Christin closed the other. Instinctively, Edith checked the gauges on the two main engines and noted that the starboard engine was running hot. She was also beginning to smell hot oil. As the ship pitched and yawed, she struggled to pull out the engine's lube oil dipstick and read it. Normally it would be difficult to read a dipstick accurately in such conditions, but in this case, it was apparent that the engine was in dire need of oil.

Christin knew what was happening and started toward a large locker at the front of the compartment, next to the ladder. "I'll get the oil and the big funnel!" she exclaimed as she opened the door to the cabinet. As she made her way back toward Edith with the large bucket of lube oil and the funnel, the ship took a huge wave and lurched. Christin lost her balance which sent the bucket of oil flying into a metal bracket, puncturing its side.

Edith grabbed the bucket after steadying herself between the two big engines and turned it on its side to minimize the amount of oil spilled. Christin was thrown back into the ladder and started writhing in agony on the deck.

Edith was terrified and lunged toward Christin. "You okay?! You hit your back hard!"

"Yeah, I think I'm okay. I don't think anything is broken but it hurts like hell! Gimme a minute and I'll see if I can work through the pain."

"You lie there, and I'll take care of the oil. We don't need you getting hurt any worse."

Edith returned to the starboard engine. She wrangled the cap from the lube oil tank and inserted the funnel, securing it in place by jamming it under the pipe that ran above it. She grabbed the punctured bucket of oil and emptied the contents into the tank through the hole in the damaged can. She threw the emptied bucket to the side and grabbed another from the locker, struggling to get it back to the engine as the ship pitched and rolled. Edith carefully worked her way around Christin, who was lying in her path. She steadied herself between a pipe and the engine by propping a leg on the lube tank to keep herself anchored. She removed the cap from the bucket's spout and emptied it into the tank. After every drop of oil was gone from the bucket, she threw it off to the side to join the other one and screwed the cap on the tank.

"That should do it!" Edith shouted to Christin as she made her way back to her. "How are you doing? Can you move?"

"I think I can make it to a rack if you help me, but it really hurts."

Edith carefully and gently ran her hands all over Christin's body and under her back to assess her condition and determine if she had any other injuries that needed tending before moving her. "I don't feel anything else out of place and I don't see any blood. I am going to try and help you to your rack, so you can rest," Edith said as she fought back tears. "This is going to hurt like hell."

"It's okay. I'm ready. Just take it slow and steady me as best you can when the ship rolls."

Edith helped Christin stand slowly and placed her arm around her neck to help support her weight. They made their way to the ladder and Edith helped Christin slowly climb the rungs until she was lying face down on the galley floor at the top of the ladder. Edith emerged after Christin, and once again helped her to roll over. "You lay here until I collapse the table and make up the rack."

A soft and tortured, "Okay," was the only reply from Christin. She lay on the floor with sweat rolling off her forehead from the intense pain she endured every time the ship rolled or shuddered.

Edith made quick work of piecing together the parts of the rack, arranging the cushions to form a bed. She then gently helped Christin lift herself onto the cushioned mattress and rolled her over on her side to examine her back. She pulled up Christin's shirt to begin a slow and methodical examination of every inch of her back for signs of serious injury.

"I don't see anything too serious, but you are going to have one hell of a bruise for a few days. I am going to strap you into the rack, so you don't roll out as we pitch around out here. I'll also get you some pain killers to help you ride out this storm a little easier."

Edith rolled Christin onto her back and then took the large hook and loop-covered straps used to secure crew members while they sleep in heavy seas and used them to secure Christin in place. She then dug a few Percocet tablets out of the first aid kit, which Christin choked down without the assistance of water.

"I'll be fine. It only hurts when I move, breathe, or think. You need to go tend to the engine room and help Rachel. The two of you are going to have to save this ship on your own."

"Okay, but I'll be back to check on you soon."

Edith planted a kiss on Christin's head and another gentle one on her lips. "I love you, sweet girl."

"I know you do. Now go."

Edith took a few steps up the ladder to the wheelhouse and hollered to Rachel, "Christin is down for the count. She's hurt bad and resting. It's just you and me, Skipper."

"Okay, I'm holding my own up here. You do your best down there and we'll make it through this."

"You got it. I'm heading down to the engine room. If you need me for anything, just chirp the general quarters alarm and I'll come running. At times like this, I wish the intercom was working better in the engine room."

"I got it. Now go!"

Edith slid down the ladder and disappeared into the engine room.

For another six hours, the storm rained its fury down on the *Lady Destiny*. When the worst had subsided, the three battered souls could only breathe a scant sigh of relief. With one crew member down, it meant that Rachel had to stay up at the helm while Edith rested a few hours before taking her turn.

After an uneventful crossing of the Gulf of Mexico and a quick, refreshing stop in Cancun, Rachel had suspected they would face some fierce weather and she hadn't been wrong. They had prepared the best they could and did everything by the book. They might be battered and bruised from their ordeal, but they weren't beaten. Whatever force was trying to end their adventure, it had failed to stop them. They were true masters of the sea and they had the scars and bruises to prove it.

Now it was just two days to the Panama Canal, and hopefully, smooth sailing ahead.

Chapter 13

BUREAUCRACY AT ITS FINEST

The *Lady Destiny* and her weathered crew arrived in Cristóbal just as dawn was breaking over the horizon. Even though the day was just beginning, the temperature was already in the mid-80s and climbing quickly. Rachel docked in a berth on the far side of the docks as Edith and Christin made short work of tying her off and hooking up the shore services after they scrounged up a few adapters to make everything fit properly.

Rachel dialed a number on her satellite phone and rested it on her shoulder while she tapped away on her computer. Over a week ago she had filed paperwork to make the canal crossing and hired an agent to get them through since it was their first time. The phone was picked up by an automated phone system with the voice of a Latina woman with a thick accent. She asked Rachel the routine volley of questions about how she would like to proceed, requiring a numbered response at each inquiry. She selected English from the choices, and then began to answer the endless string of questions about her request for transit confirmation numbers, hull number, point of origin, country of registration, and so on. After nearly 40 minutes, she completed the automated arrival questionnaire. The computerized paperwork was also submitted with a few quick keystrokes. Now, all they could do was wait for the agent to arrive. Luckily, they had arrived a good eight hours early, despite all they had been through.

About four hours later, the agent's representative arrived. He was tall, thin, darkly tanned, and well-weathered with dark hair and eyes. He wore blue shorts, a captain's hat, and a white shirt with the company's logo embroidered on the front. He stood at the edge of the *Lady Destiny II* and yelled at her with a British accent as if expecting the ship to answer him directly. "Permission to come aboard, Captain?"

Rachel slid back the window and hollered down, "Permission granted. Welcome aboard."

The man responded in kind with a look of surprise and astonishment at being addressed by a woman on a fishing trawler. Once he gained his composure and accepted the oddity of the situation, he crossed over to the boat with the grace of a ballerina. He landed firmly and soundly on the slowly rocking deck. He proceeded to the wheelhouse where he removed his cap and addressed Rachel.

"Am I to presume that you are Rachel Kristiansen and that you are the captain of this vessel?

"I am," she responded proudly.

"I must apologize. I was not expecting you to be the captain. I assumed you were the admin for a fishing company and had submitted the paperwork on behalf of the captain and filled out the forms incorrectly. I see now that everything is in order. I am Jonathan Rakes and I will be your agency representative for your crossings."

"Nice to meet you, Jonathan. I'm Rachel, and the two ladies you see on the deck are my crew. Edith has black hair and Christin is the redhead. I must apologize as well; I expected to be greeted by a Panamanian national, not a Brit."

"I retired after twenty years in the Queen's Navy. I had been this way several times during my career and decided to settle here at my retirement. This job is just something I do to bring in a little extra money and give me something to do. I don't want to end up like so many others around here who fritter away their remaining years drinking in local bars and dying of liver disease."

"Well, we are glad to have you aboard. Have all the arrangements been made for our crossing?"

"Most have been made. Let me tell you how things will progress from this point onward through the crossing."

"I'm all ears, but let's go down below to the galley where it's cooler and where we can sit in relative comfort."

"Lead the way, Captain."

Rachel led the way down the access ladder. She took a seat at the galley table and gestured to Jonathan to do the same. "Can I offer you anything to eat or drink? We have water, soft drinks, and coffee."

"I'll take bottled water, please." After Edith handed him the cold water, Jonathan nodded his thanks and began speaking. "I must say, you keep a clean ship. I can smell the remnants of previous catches but not like I have on other vessels I've encountered."

"We try to keep things clean and tidy. The girls do a great job and they take a lot of pride in this boat. She may be a bit rusty and in need of some paint, but for a large part of the year she's home to us, and we like her to be comfortable."

"You have my admiration for your leadership abilities

and the dedication of your crew. I'm glad to see the world is changing."

Jonathan continued. "Now, about the crossing. Since you have not made a canal crossing before, you will be required to undergo an inspection and measurement by the canal operators to show seaworthiness and suitability for the crossing. I'm sure you have read that there are many guidelines for crossing the canal that must be met before you can obtain a final crossing authorization. I see in your paperwork that this vessel is under 128 feet long, so you will most likely need to be handlined through the canal. If the canal authority does require handlining, you will be required to have up to four linemen, excuse me, line persons, onboard along with a crossing advisor or pilot. These personnel will be assigned by our agency and you will be required to pay the fees outlined in the paperwork. Do you understand this?"

"I do. I have reviewed the rules and I believe we should have no problem with the inspection."

"Very well. We have you on the schedule for the inspection, so you should expect to have someone stop by within the next three days."

"Three days?!" Rachel exclaimed.

"Yes. Normal time to inspection after arriving in port is two to three days. Since we are working as your agent, we will handle the details and try to have someone here as soon as possible, but I cannot make any guarantees."

"I guess that will have to work. I will just send the girls into town to get a few things and we can make a few repairs while we're docked."

At that moment Edith and Christin entered the galley covered in sweat. Christin piped in, "Boy, it's hot enough to steam oysters out there."

Jonathan stood as the ladies entered.

"This is Jonathan Rakes. He will be our transit agent for the canal crossing. Jonathan, this is Edith and Christin."

"I'm very pleased to meet you both." He shook their hands firmly as if testing their mettle. After shaking both their hands, he nodded and smiled with approval. "I see you are a strong and competent crew."

"We are the best, Johnny. Just ask Rachel," Edith replied.

In a terse tone, the slender man corrected her. "The name is Jonathan, and Rachel has informed me of your abilities. Now, we do have one detail to take care of that involves all of you. Since you will be departing the boat and entering the country while you are docked here, I must stamp your passports to allow you entry. Since you are ship's crew, your visas have prior approval."

Edith reached into a locker above the pantry cabinet to retrieve the passports and handed them to Jonathan.

"These all look to be in order, but be aware that Christin's passport is about to expire in eight months. Some countries will not allow you to enter if you are within six months of expiration."

"No problem there. We have to be back in Gloucester before then for the fishing season."

"Very well. I've stamped your passports and you are free to enter the country for the next ten days." Jonathan turned toward the crew. "Thank you, captain and crew. I bid you farewell for now and I will be in touch." He turned and found his way out the side door of the galley and onto the deck. He was across the docks in an instant.

"Hey, Rachel, ain't he a bit of a stuffed shirt? He needs a blowjob more than any man I know."

"Yeah, I know. He just spent too many years in the 'Queen's Navy,' and he does it all by the book. Right now, we need to play nice since our crossing is in his hands."

Later that night, the three women lay sleeping in their racks. It was truly a rare event for all three women to be able to sleep at the same time and the fold-out galley bed was a bit cramped with three bodies sprawled across it, but it was all they could do since they removed the extra bunks a couple of years earlier to make room for more storage and a proper shower. Christin was sleeping with a smile across her face, as she had Rachel enveloped against the outer bulkhead which meant that Rachel had to sleep spooned against her. The pressure of Rachel's body against Christin's still annoyingly sore back gave her comfort even in their current state of discomfort.

A loud banging sound came from outside the galley. Rachel was startled awake and jumped up, hitting her head against a light fixture that hung about a foot above her.

"Dammit! That hurt."

Rachel grabbed a small pistol from the shelf next to her as she shuffled her way over to Edith and Christin in a series of comical motions. Wearing little more than panties and a loose-fitting tank top, Rachel swung open the door violently, nearly knocking a shadowy figure over the side of the ship. Edith and Christin scrambled behind her.

"Who are you?! What do you want and what are you doing here?!" she shouted.

In a thick Panamanian accent, a scratchy voice replied, "Pardon, ma'am, pardon, ma'am. I do not mean to intrude. I am here to inspect your vessel."

Rachel lowered her pistol and in an apologetic tone, she replied, "I am sorry, but we did not expect you for a couple more days. We thought we would be told when you were coming aboard, and the inspection would be done during daylight hours."

"My apologies. We work all hours and most vessels do

not completely shut down when in port, so I did not expect to wake you. When I saw that your vessel was captained by a woman, I wanted to be sure to do your inspection."

"That's a bit chauvinistic but I'll let it slide. What can we do to help you?"

"There is nothing I need at this time. But I would like your engineer to accompany me on the inspection."

"That's Edith. She's the one with black hair."

The inspector reached out his hand to Edith as she rubbed her eyes and adjusted her tank top which had gotten twisted as she slept, allowing a nipple to become exposed through an armhole. She grabbed his hand firmly and shook it as she smothered a yawn. "Okay, let's get this over with."

Edith slipped on a pair of flip flops as Rachel and Christin settled down on the edge of the rack with a couple of bottled waters. The inspector and Edith disappeared through the galley door and out onto the deck.

For nearly two hours, Edith and the inspector moved methodically through the boat before finally returning to the galley.

"Thank you, ladies. I have all the information I need. I will turn in the paperwork and you should hear back from Canal Authority Operations within two days once they have granted your vessel clearance to transit."

Rachel rose from her position on the rack. "Thank you, very much. If you need anything else, let me know."

The inspector turned to her with an outstretched hand. "I will. Thank you again, Captain. It was my pleasure to be your inspector." He turned and exited through the door, and disappeared down the dimly lit dock into the night.

The three women were now more exhausted than they were when they first retired earlier in the evening. They piled back into their positions on the cramped rack and returned to their slumbers.

The next morning started very much like the one before: hot and humid. Edith was back in the engine room before the others awoke, tending to one of the two air conditioning units that wasn't quite doing its job. Rachel came up behind her. "Whatcha doing?"

"I couldn't sleep very well cramped up on the bunk, so I decided to come back here and fashion a hammock from some netting. Also, the number one A/C unit isn't cooling right, so I'm going to use the downtime to fix it. Looks like it just needs some refrigerant. I'll have to go into town and see if I can find some. I have plenty for the cargo hold coolers, but this is a different type."

"Sounds good. Let's get as much repair work done as we can while we're waiting. I have a feeling that those A/C units will be very important from here on out. You better get some oil for the engines, too, since we went through so much in the storm. By the way, did you find out why we burned all that oil?"

"We were being tossed around a lot and with the higher temperatures, the oil seems to have gotten thin. It looks like it was blowing past the valves and rings and burning off in the engine. I don't think there's any damage, but I used the rest of the oil to refill the tank. I'll get a couple of buckets when I'm ashore."

Rachel entered the galley and found Christin standing at the stove. "I guess your back is feeling better. What are you making? It smells great."

"My back is much better. A little sore and bruised but it isn't going to keep me down. I was talking to some of the locals while we were in Cancun and I got some great recipes using the local foods. I'm making fried plantains and folding them into crepes. Then, I'm covering them with a vanilla, cinnamon, and bourbon glaze reduction with fresh guava juice and some tasajo, which is dried red meat that I put a spicy glaze on."

"Sounds wonderful! I love it when you do the cooking. You can make chicken salad out of chicken shit and everyone loves it. And you always try new tastes, we never get bored."

"If you want to call Edith, it should be ready in a couple of minutes."

Rachel headed back to where she had just come from and found Edith washing her hands to remove the grease and grime. "Breakfast is ready, Edith. Come on up and eat."

"I'm on my way. Lead on."

Just as Rachel turned around, Edith slapped her firmly on the ass, making a loud crack. Rachel shook her head and continued walking.

The three gathered around the galley table, said a short prayer, and set in on Christin's delicious breakfast.

"Give me one more crepe and I have to get into town," Edith announced, as she reached across the table for the juice.

"Just make sure you put on your bra. We don't need you showing off and getting in trouble."

"Okay, Mother Christin."

Edith stuffed in her last mouthful of crepe, making her look like an overstuffed chipmunk. She stood up and whipped off her tank top.

"Dang, are you just gonna strip down in front of Rachel, right here?"

"Cool it, we're among friends and we all have the same gear. Besides, it's not like these tank tops and bikinis leave a lot to the imagination, anyway. As hot as it is, I'd go naked if I could."

"Just get dressed and get going while we take care of everything here," Christin said with a smirk.

Edith strapped on her bra and put her top back on. "Okay, I'm gone. If you don't hear from me in two hours, send the Coast Guard."

Edith gave Christin a quick kiss and bolted through the door, leaving the two to finish breakfast and take care of the boat.

After breakfast, Rachel headed out to town to meet with the transit agency and settle the final details regarding their crossing. Rachel spent over an hour with the transit agency's representative. Before departing, the agency rep shook her hand and offered a small token. "Enjoy your time crossing the canal and take many pictures. On behalf of our transit agency, I would like to present this gift basket to you and your crew. It has been a pleasure doing business with you. Now, if you will sign these releases and the fee schedule locking in your charges, we will complete everything and give you a call once we have received authorization to transit."

"Great! Thank you for making this crossing so efficient. I don't think I could have done it by myself, and I can't afford any delays."

"That is our job, Captain. We have already begun the paperwork for your return passage and will fill in the dates once we hear from you. Just give us a two-day notice and we will put you on the schedule, but remember that the large ships always take priority over smaller vessels and pleasure craft."

"Alright. Thanks again."

Rachel exited the office and turned the corner onto the

street leading to the docks. As she came to the next intersection, she nearly ran over Edith pushing a cart full of drums and barrels.

"Hey! Everything okay?"

"Yeah, took me all day, but I found everything we need. Had to pay a hefty price too. They know you need it and they can get it for you, but you gotta pay their price. It's almost like everything here is handled through the black market. Hell, they even made me buy this rickety old cart to haul it in since they won't deliver anything. Of course, you know that once we're gone, they'll just come and get the damn thing and sell it to the next poor sucker."

"I know. It's fine. We should have everything we need for a while and we can chalk this up to experience."

"Okay, please, help me push this thing. One of the wheels rubs a bit making it even harder than it already is. These old beat-up roads don't help, either."

Twenty minutes later the women arrived at the boat and loaded the supplies. Christin had just finished cleaning out the strainers and checked all the systems. She was getting ready to go into town and get food supplies. Fresh food and good meals do more for crew morale than any booze or entertainment.

Rachel placed the gift basket on the galley table and opened it. Inside she found a bottle of Seco Herrerano, a Panamanian liquor used in mixed drinks; a bottle of local rum, Carte Vieja; three Panama hats made in Ecuador; a Panamanian soccer team jersey; a small Panamanian flag; and, three pounds of Panamanian coffee.

"Wow, what a great gift! That was nice of the transit agency," Rachel said, absolutely amazed at the basket's bounty.

Edith stated, "I'm heading back to the A/C unit to

charge it up. I want to check the batteries and replace that aux pump motor we burned up, too."

"You need a hand?" Rachel inquired.

"Nah, I got it. You go with Christin and make sure she doesn't get into any trouble. It can be a bit rough in town."

"Alright, we'll head into town. I'll lock the hatches while we're gone, so you aren't rudely interrupted by a curious local who might want to cause trouble."

"That's fine. See you ladies later."

Rachel and Christin made their way into town and found a small market area where they purchased plantains, preserved pork, rice, yucca, tortillas, a sack full of fresh empanadas from a street vendor, other various foodstuffs, and a large container of Perry Bay stew, a hearty fish stew perfect for keeping back winter's chill.

They returned to the ship to find Edith lounging on the deck in a bikini with a large glass of scotch over ice.

"So, I take it you got everything done?"

"You bet. I even fixed the turbo that overheated and the ice maker. Now we can have cold drinks and margaritas made the right way. By the way, the transit agency called, and we have clearance. The transit advisor will be on board around 10:00 a.m. tomorrow to prepare and make sure the fenders are installed properly. So, once you guys are done putting up the groceries, I need help putting that stack of tires around the ship."

"Sure, give us a minute," replied Christin.

The next morning at 10:00 a.m. sharp, Jonathan and the handlining crewmen arrived on board to prepare for the transit. The men handled the work effortlessly as they methodically attended to every detail on their checklist.

Lady Destiny entered the transit route around 1:00 p.m.

and they would join five other vessels in the massive locks to transit together.

The entire transit took a little more than nine hours from the Atlantic side to the Pacific side. Nothing eventful happened outside of a few whistles and catcalls from the linemen working on the locks who reveled at the sight of a vessel crewed by women.

When they emerged in Balboa, they docked at a small pier. Rachel signed the necessary paperwork and watched Jonathan and his crewmen depart to the docks, leaving them fend for themselves and remove the old fender tires that had been installed in Cristóbal. Rachel hired a couple of locals working on the dock to help them out with stacking the tires neatly on the dock and accounting for all of them. They cast off once more toward their final destiny, all but disappearing into the night except for their mast and running lights.

Chapter 14

FAIR WINDS AND FOLLOWING SEAS

Rachel sat back in her command chair as they glided smoothly through the darkness. She used the time to contemplate what had brought them together for this quest.

Growing up in Gloucester was a wonderful experience for Rachel. She spent most of her time living with her mother's parents since they had a housekeeper to help with keeping an eye on her. Her father stayed with his mother, Gramma Gwen, in her small stone house near the docks. He didn't really need a home since he spent so much time at sea. He enjoyed staying with his mother since his father had died of heart failure so many years earlier. He knew there were many times when she was lonely and could use the extra company.

Rachel's maternal grandparents lived in a large home a bit further from the docks in an affluent neighborhood. She had her own room with a fancy canopy bed and plenty of toys, none of which fit her personality. Rachel was a tomboy, through and through. Most days after school, when she wasn't at Gwen's house, she could be found in the back yard, climbing the elm tree and hanging from its branches with the neighbor girl.

Rachel's best friend lived in the elegant large house next door. A thick hedge completely separated the two properties except for a small gate in the back yard. The girls were two of a kind. When they played hide and seek, Rachel never had a problem finding the little girl from over the hedge. Her long, curly, bright red hair stood out like a sore thumb and was impossible to hide. Christin loved Rachel and they were seldom apart. They went to school together, played together, went to the docks together, and every chance they had, they visited Gramma Gwen.

Gwen worked for the local cannery until her retirement. It paid well and she was able to build a hefty nest egg which allowed her to enjoy a comfortable retirement. She worked the day shift and would get home in the evening around 4:30. Nearly every day, Rachel and Christin would be waiting for her on the sofa in the living room. They were always excited to eat dinner together. After dinner, they would do homework, swap stories, and wait for Rachel's father to get home on those days when he was able to return from sea.

After Gwen fully retired and Rachel's father had passed on, the two girls spent more and more time down at the little stone house. They loved keeping Gwen company and there were always plenty of things to do. Gwen had no trouble making time for them and she cherished every moment they had together. They would play board games, ride bikes around town, and explore the craggy coastline around the harbor near the lighthouse.

More memories came pouring back into Rachel's mind as she sat back in her chair and fell into a lull with nothing to accompany her except the moon, stars, the sounds of the waves beating against the hull, and the roar of the engines under her feet.

Rachel had a hard time adjusting to high school without her father to support her, but she did her best and made good grades. She didn't have many friends except for Christin but that was enough. Rachel found most of the other students immature and at best, a distraction. Christin, on the other hand, had many friends during the school day and several boyfriends, but her evenings were usually dedicated to spending time with Rachel and Gwen. They were a family in every sense of the word. Gwen loved the girls and they loved her.

Their senior year, Rachel and Christin both moved out of their homes to live with Gwen. Heck, most of the time outside of school they could be found in the modest stone house anyway, so it was inevitable. The girls each had a small room upstairs and Gwen had the big room at the end of the hallway.

A couple of nights a week, Christin would go out with her boyfriend of the week and leave Rachel and Gwen to share valuable one-on-one time. On the weekends, if there wasn't much going on, the girls would join Pete on his boat as part of his crew to learn the art of fishing and good seamanship.

On Pete's boat, they were treated like everyone else with no special considerations. They were forced to pull their weight and carry an equal share of the burden and when they didn't, they heard about it. In return, they gained valuable knowledge and a good wage to help them through school, even though neither of them needed to worry about money.

Through thick and thin, rain, sun, and stormy seas, they worked hard. Rachel had a special knack for fishing and was a welcomed part of the crew, even though many of the superstitious crewmen viewed women on a boat as a curse. She learned everything she could about navigation, engineering, fishing, ship repair, and leadership.

On one spring day, Christin skipped out of school in the early afternoon. She quietly snuck out to her car. As she reached for the door handle, someone grabbed her from behind and spun her around aggressively, throwing her against the driver's door. It was Alan, her now ex-boyfriend. He had quite a temper and was prone to violence. He didn't like the fact that Christin had broken up with him the night before. She had gone home with bruises on her arms several times before and she'd had enough. Although Christin had made it clear that they were through, Alan was not ready to let her go. He pinned both of her shoulders against the car so she couldn't move or defend herself.

"Alan! I have nothing to say to you!"

"Yeah, well, I have plenty to say to you! You don't break up with me! I own you and you don't do anything unless I say you can."

"Alan, you never owned me. I just let you tag along until I saw what kind of an asshole you were. That's why I broke up with you. I will not be treated like a piece of property, and you've disrespected and hurt me for the last time! Now, leave me alone!"

"Oh! I'm not done with you, yet."

"I'm done with you, so let go of me and leave me alone!" Christin struggled to free herself from Alan's firm grasp.

"You're not going anywhere!" he exclaimed, as he removed one hand from her shoulder and drew back to strike her.

In his preparations for an onslaught of violence and rage, he failed to notice the figure approaching from behind. Just as he started to bring his fist forward, the person grabbed his arm and yanked him backward. The next thing he felt was a knee to the groin. He fell to the ground, groaning and writhing in agony. As he lay there moaning, he felt crushing blows being delivered to his face as someone's black combat boots made several attempts to inflict serious damage.

Through his bloody and swollen eye, he saw Christin appear. She reared back with her right foot and kicked him squarely in the ribs twice. She peered down at his battered body and uttered one word, "ASSHOLE!"

Christin turned to her rescuer. She did not know who the person standing before her dressed all in black was, but she had seen her around the school many times. "Thank you! You saved me from a maniac who would have really hurt me."

The dark figure responded in a throaty female drone, "No problem, I don't think you'll have any more problems out of him as long as he's learned his lesson and if he hasn't, we can keep him after class for some private tutoring."

Christin locked her car door, and then turned to her rescuer. Together the pair walked back to the school leaving Alan alone to deal with his injuries and embarrassment. After all, he'd just been beaten up by a girl.

"I've seen you around. You're usually hanging out with the kids on the corner, skipping class and smoking," she said to the girl in black.

"Yeah, I know. School's just way too easy and it bores me. I can't stand to sit in a class all day and listen to people who only want to hear themselves talk. To be honest, I couldn't give a flip about anyone else's ideas."

"By the way, I'm Christin." She held out her hand.

"I'm Edith," she responded, as she grabbed the girl's hand.

"Thank you, again. You can really handle yourself."

"That was mostly luck. I caught him off guard, but I have been known to throw a punch or two. I've noticed you, too. I've seen you walking around school and at some of the ball games with your boyfriends. It's hard to miss your beautiful red hair."

"Thanks, I like it, too. It's an unmanageable mess today."

"I don't think so. I think it looks great." Edith reached her hand up and ran her fingers through Christin's hair. With a smile, she reached out and hugged Christin. "You're going to be fine now. I'll help you with anything that you can't handle."

Christin returned the hug and whispered in Edith's ear, "I won't need your protection anymore, but I would like your friendship."

"You bet, girl! Always and forever."

The rest of the year passed without incident. Edith joined Pete's crew and dug into the work. Right away everyone knew she was a natural when it came to the sea, mechanics, and engineering.

As the school year progressed and came to an end, the girls became best friends. Their time together was magical but also bittersweet because the time came for each of them to find their own way in the world.

Pete helped Edith to secure a huge scholarship to the Marine Maritime Academy in Castine, Maine. This was a wonderful blessing for Edith since her family was poor and she was living with her single mother who struggled to make a living and keep a roof over their heads. Pete was like a father to Edith and he believed in her natural abilities, so he helped her in any way that he could. In return, Edith studied hard and completed her master's degree in marine engineering in only four and a half years by attending summer sessions and taking a full load of classes each semester.

Christin and Rachel both attended Boston College; however, Rachel quit after just two years. She concluded that college wasn't for her. She couldn't handle the hustle and bustle around her and the pressure of learning while being surrounded by the constant distractions of college life. She had two boyfriends in those two years and neither one lasted for more than a month. It seemed that no man could handle Rachel's strong will, determination, and the maturity that came with being a woman of the sea. She didn't seem to like the notion of being anchored to anyone else. She valued her freedom and independence.

Christin completed school with a bachelor's degree in business management. It wasn't her first choice in academics, but it was the wishes of her parents. They wanted her to follow in their footsteps and eventually take over the family's international shipping and trading business.

After dropping out of school, Rachel moved back to Gloucester with Gwen and took a job on Pete's boat. It was a natural transition and one of the few places she felt comfortable. Many times, she thought to herself, *If I could wake up each day and feel the salt spray stinging my face, I think I could be eternally happy.*

As time passed, Rachel advanced her knowledge and eventually got her captain's certificate. She continued to work on Pete's boat, but now she had a new goal. She wanted to buy her own boat and ride the ocean currents, harvesting the bounty of the sea as her father did.

Christin went to work for her parents in the family business. She had a fine office with a window overlooking the docks and harbor. She kept a pair of binoculars on the windowsill and she would watch for Pete's boat every day. She would scan the horizon, always praying that they would return safely and bring her best friend back to her. She was often bored and never seemed to get much accomplished at work; this caused tension between her and her father. She was always distracted by the sea and had a constant desire to seek out adventure, but at the time Pete didn't have any room on his crew and if she left the company, she was afraid it would destroy her mother. Every evening, Christin would stop by Gwen's house to check on her as she grabbed a beer and a quick bite.

Gwen could always sense Christin's internal turmoil. "Christin, when are you going to follow your dreams and find happiness? Your parents' paths aren't your own, you know."

"Yeah, I know. But I don't want to destroy what I have with my family."

"What makes you think that your happiness will ruin your relationship with your family? I bet if you talked to them and explained your feelings, they would understand and support you."

"I know you're right, but it's hard when they've had my life planned for me since I was a little girl."

"Give them a chance and they just might surprise you."

At that moment Rachel burst through the door. She ran to Gwen and planted a huge kiss on her cheek. "Hey, Grams, what's for dinner?"

Next, she turned to Christin and planted another big kiss on her cheek. "Good Lord, you smell like fish!" Christin blurted out.

"Oh, you know you like it. I call it *Eau du Poisson*."

"It fits. Now go get cleaned up before you ruin my dress."

"Yeah, yeah, I hear ya. Hey, Grams, I just saw that the *Eiger* is up for sale. I'm going to talk to them tomorrow."

"That's great. You've wanted your own boat for some time now and you've saved a good down payment."

"Yep, but I don't know if it will be enough for the bank to give me a loan since I don't have much credit."

"How much do need?" Christin inquired.

"Rumor has it they want $470,000 for it, but I know it needs some work, so I think I can get it for considerably less. The only other problem is finding a crew. Not too many people are willing to work for a female captain."

"Don't worry about that. When people are hungry and need to put food on the table, they'll work for anyone."

"Yeah, but I want a crew like the one we had when we all worked together on Pete's boat."

"One day you will get your crew, but you can't get a crew without a boat."

The next day, Rachel spent a good portion of the day negotiating a price for the boat. She had free time while Pete was having his starboard engine repaired. She had a firm price by 10:30 a.m. which wasn't quite as low as she wanted, but good boats were hard to find, and the owner knew it. She also had three bank rejections by 4:00 p.m.

Rachel sat, dejected, at the table in Gwen's house. At 4:30, the door swung open and Christin walked in with a huge smile on her face. "Honey, I'm home."

"Hey, Christin. Looks like you had a good day?"

"I did. I had a long meeting today with my mother and father. I told them what I wanted to do with my life."

"What's that?" Rachel asked, with one eyebrow cocked up and a smirk that lit up her face.

"I told them I want to own a fishing boat."

Rachel busted out laughing uncontrollably. Between giggles and snorts, she managed to get a few words out. "Why would you want to do that? You don't have a captain's license, and no one will sell you a boat without one."

"No, they won't, but I know the business side of things and I know they will sell you one. So, what do you say, partner?"

"Partner? I don't remember asking for a partner. Also, what makes you think I need a partner?"

"I know you had some trouble at the banks today. You know my father has the pulse of business in this town and he knows all about any developments that might impact him, like, say, the potential for a new boat bringing its haul into the cannery," Christin said slyly.

"You don't have enough money either and the banks won't finance me."

"No, I don't have enough, but I have $50,000 saved up and with your $100,000 we have one hell of a down payment."

At that moment, Gwen rounded the corner from the bathroom, and said, "If you girls are serious, I may be able to help. I have a little extra saved up for retirement that isn't doing much in the market right now. If you can get me a return on my investment, you can have it."

Rachel quickly rebuffed the idea. "No! I can't do that. You need that money."

"No, I don't. I have everything I need. I also have my pension from the cannery. You need the money more than I do. Do you think you can stand having a crotchety old fool for a partner? If you'll let me, I want to help you both fulfill your dreams."

Christin chimed in, "I would love having you as a partner, but it's up to Rachel."

"How much are we talking, Grams?"

"Oh, after thirty-two years of hard work, I have a little disposable savings. How does $75,000 sound?"

"Wait! What? Really? You would do that for us?"

"Yes. I would give my life if it meant your happiness."

"Well, that puts us at $225,000. But they will only take $400,000, so we are still short $175,000."

Christin leaned back from the table with a devious grin and a bounce. "As the business-minded part of this outfit, you leave that to me. We have a destiny to buy this boat."

"That's it! We will name her the *Lady Destiny II,* after my father's boat. It **is** our destiny."

The next morning around 10:00 a.m., Rachel could see Christin walking down the dock toward Pete's boat, which was still undergoing repairs. She had a spring in her step and a grin on her face.

"So, what are you smiling about?" Rachel asked with apprehension.

"It's ours," Christin replied.

"What is?"

"The *Lady Destiny*."

"What do you mean!? It's ours?"

"Easy. I quit my job, pulled my savings out of the bank, and talked my father into financing the remainder of the loan at four percent interest over six years. All you have to do is sign the document in my briefcase."

"You're shitting me!! That isn't funny, Christin."

"I wouldn't shit you; you're my favorite turd. Now, come on up here and let's go get our boat."

"What about the repairs and a crew?"

"I have that covered, too. I got Mom to throw a little bit of secret capital in on the deal, with no strings attached, and then I contacted a first-rate engineer to join our crew."

"That's great, but where did you find a first-rate engineer we can afford? You don't know anyone."

"I made a call last night and she'll be here in about two hours."

"She??? You don't mean…"

"Yep, Edith is on her way. Like the Blues Brothers said, 'We're putting the band back together.'"

"Boy, you really do know the business side of things. Okay, let's go get our boat."

That evening the three women spent time with Gwen and it was like they'd never parted ways. The same old love and feelings for one another just came rushing in.

"Now that we have a boat, the work is really going to begin. I'll go down tomorrow, assess her condition, and see what I can start overhauling," Edith said.

"That would be awesome, Edith. I'll meet you early in the morning, while Christin takes care of the final paperwork."

Gwen sat quietly in her rocking chair with a big smile across her face as tears silently rolled down her cheeks, leaving salty streaks. "I love you, girls, and I am so happy for you. I want to thank you for letting me be a part of this."

"Aww, we couldn't have done it without you, Grams," Christin said, as she reached over and hugged Gwen while wiping the tears from her eyes.

"So, it's settled. Now I just need a place to crash for the night before I head down to the docks. Would you mind if I stayed here, Gwen?" asked Edith.

"Of course not. You are all are welcome to spend the night here," Gwen said.

"Actually, Edith's going to stay with me at my apartment. I have room and she once did a huge favor for me that I haven't repaid."

"That would be great, Christin. I'd love to catch up on things."

The following morning was foggy and damp. Rachel was chipping paint down at the boat by 6:30 a.m. after a sleepless night, and Edith was nowhere to be seen. Finally, around 9:30, Edith's distinctive silhouette could be seen emerging from the gloomy mist.

"You're late!" Rachel said grumpily.

"I know. Christin and I had a lot of catching up to do and we had a long, enjoyable night."

"No excuses, just get to work."

Edith stood at attention and popped a proper salute. "Aye, aye. Captain!"

Rachel smiled and went back to work thinking how wonderful those words sounded as they rang through her ears and settled into the depths of her soul. Now they were all in it for the long haul and she was their captain…

As the past faded from her mind's eye, she once more became excited about this wonderful new adventure. They had experienced immense excitement and magnificent vistas. It had been harrowing at times, but it had always been exquisite. It was amazing to watch, as each new chapter of their lives was unveiled before them.

They emerged from the Panama Canal and traveled for a full day toward Cocos. Now, they would see their first sunset over a new horizon, a new ocean, and a new world.

Rachel reached for the intercom. "Hey, ladies, come up here. Let's watch our first Pacific sunset together."

Edith and Christin emerged from the lower compartment and sidled up to Rachel in her chair. They both had a hand on Rachel's chair to steady themselves and a hand in each of the other's back pockets.

"Isn't it beautiful?"

Christin and Edith shared a romantic kiss. "It sure is, Rachel," Christin replied.

The trio looked out the front windows of the wheelhouse at the disappearing sun. As the final sliver of light dipped below the horizon, the three were met by a brilliant flash of green light.

Rachel exclaimed, "Did you see that?! That was the green ray, the 'Eye of Odin.' It's a sign and a good omen. We are going to have 'fair winds and following seas,' from here on out. We have the blessing of Odin himself."

Chapter 15

SLEEPING WITH THE FISHES

That night, none of the girls slept well. Rachel was up in the wheelhouse massaging her temples and keeping her eyes closed as much as possible. A moment later, Edith appeared behind her from the depths of the ship.

"Hey, Rachel, you okay?"

"Yeah, I'm good. I just have this splitting headache and my ears won't stop ringing. I guess all these years of constant boat noise are finally taking a toll on my hearing."

Edith responded with a note of surprise. "That's odd. Christin and I are having the same issues and we haven't gotten a wink of sleep all night. Heck, Christin won't even let me cuddle with her. The ringing is driving us crazy and I've been back to the engine room and out on deck three times. I can't figure out what's causing it or even where it could be coming from. It seems to be coming from everywhere at once with no obvious source to be found anywhere. No matter where I go it's just as loud as ever."

"Well, we can't all be suffering from acute tinnitus. I

noticed it right at sunset and it started out very soft, just a little irritating, sort of like you and Christin fighting. At first, I chalked it up to water in my ears, but it keeps getting stronger with every passing moment."

"Ha, you are so funny when you are in pain and bitchy," Edith said with a scowl.

"It's hard to be funny right now with this headache."

"You want an aspirin or something?"

"I took four a few minutes ago."

A moment later, Christin sauntered into the cabin looking exhausted and three ways of pissed off.

"Are you both hearing that annoying sound? I can see on Rachel's face that she must be hearing it, too. I put earplugs in and earmuffs from the engine room over the top of those and it made no difference. It feels like the sound is coming from inside my head and carries above everything else."

"I haven't tried earplugs yet," Rachel blurted out.

"Don't bother. The only thing they do is clear the sound up a bit. It seems to have a faint melody, like a choir singing an aria together."

"I don't care what it is, I just want this shit to stop before I lose my mind."

The three sat in the wheelhouse for several more hours without speaking. They clasped their hands over their ears and winced in pain as the sound became louder and louder.

They stared out across the water as the sun broke over the horizon on their starboard side.

Edith yelled, "Do you guys hear that?!"

"Yeah! Silence, at last," Christin whispered, as tears of pain ran down her cheeks and hung on her strong jawline.

"That was freaking weird. I hope it doesn't come back again."

"You said it, Rachel. Christin and I are going below to do the morning checks. When we are done, I will come up and relieve you for a while, so you can rest."

"Thanks. I sure could use a couple hours of sleep. Let's do two-hour rotations, so we can all get a bit of sleep, in short order."

"I'll be back in a blink. Just hang tight for a few more minutes."

Edith and Christin disappeared below, and Rachel was left alone with the autopilot. Almost immediately she began to doze off in her chair.

As her vision began slipping through the gray spectrum to the black of sleep, Rachel began to dream. Not a dream of great visions but of swirling colors and indiscernible shapes. Just as the colors washed over her, she heard a voice whisper, "Rachel, my love."

Rachel eyes immediately flew open and she sat up straight in her chair. She glanced around to see Edith poking her head in.

"What did you say?" Rachel asked her skeptically.

"I didn't say anything. I was just coming up to relieve you. Gimme the chair and you go catch a few winks while you can."

"Okay, I will. Autopilot is set and we are making about 15 knots toward the island."

"Aye, aye, Cap'n. Now get your ass outta my chair."

"Yes, ma'am. See you in a few."

Rachel disappeared below, where she found Christin lying naked on the galley rack sound asleep. A small amount of drool was making its way from the corner of her mouth to her pillow.

During the layover in Panama, Edith reconfigured the galley area so there were now two separate racks and a hammock for them to sleep in, instead of one large, cramped rack. This made things much more comfortable in the heat; now they wouldn't have to pile up together. Christin claimed the one right next to the access hatch that led up to the wheelhouse.

She must have taken a shower and fallen asleep as soon as her head hit the pillow, Rachel thought to herself. *Poor gal, I put you through so much.* Rachel bent over and kissed her on the forehead as she whispered, "Thank you, Christin. I love you so much."

Rachel lay down on her rack just opposite Christin and stared at the ceiling. She followed the contours of the cracks in the paint like she always did when she needed to fall asleep quickly. The eerie voice she'd heard during her dream kept playing through her mind. Finally, after what seemed like an eternity, she drifted off to sleep as the colors once again began to swirl in her mind.

After what seemed to be mere moments, Rachel was awoken by her alarm. She wiped her eyes and tried to compose herself as she sat on the edge of her rack. She slipped on a pair of shorts and marched to the coffee pot. Her eyes stung as if filled with sand. She took a long gulp of lukewarm coffee as she walked toward the wheelhouse.

She passed by Edith's hammock where she lay snoring. Rachel reached out her hand and ran it through Edith's coal-black hair. She managed a tight smile and took another sip of her coffee as she commenced her journey back to the command chair.

She found Christin sitting in the captain's chair with her feet propped up on the console. She was only wearing a bikini and set of headphones, which barely stayed in place as she thrashed her head around in beat with the music.

Rachel reached out a hand and tapped Christin's shoulder, which immediately threw her into a terrified panic.

"You scared the shit outta me, Rach!"

"Sorry, I just wanted to let you know I was here to relieve you."

"I appreciate that, but that is not the way I wanna die."

Rachel chuckled. "Get out of my chair and go rest."

"Nag, nag, nag, that's all you do."

Christin got out of the chair and collected her things. When she was finally ready, she grabbed a coffee cup she filled with candy wrappers, pistachio nutshells, sunflower seed shells, and a banana peel that went into the trash.

"You are the queen of eating, aren't you?" Rachel quipped.

"Don't you know it, but without my cooking, you two would starve," Christin said with some annoyance.

Rachel settled into her chair and slapped Christin's ass as she turned away, making a loud smacking sound and leaving a distinct handprint on her slightly sunburned skin.

"I'll get you for that! By the way, we are about two hours out from the island. I suspect we should see it on the horizon any minute. I'm headed out to the deck to work on my tan."

"Isn't that a little hard when you are covered in SPF 70, Rachel?"

"With my skin, I could get a sunburn in the moonlight covered in chocolate under a blanket."

"I must say, it sure does bring out your freckles."

"I know. Damn those things, but they are who I am."

"Well, I think they're beautiful."

Christin closed the door to the cabin and headed forward. She set a towel in the small space near the anchor capstan and lay down to relax. She glanced in at Rachel and gave a quick wink as she lowered her sunglasses.

Rachel stared briefly at Christin's already sweaty figure. As she lifted her eyes, she could see a faint object appearing on the distant horizon in front of the bow. Once again, the noise and agonizing headache returned to torment her thoughts and permeate her psyche. This time the level of torture instantly threatened her very sanity.

Chapter 16

ENDLESS CIRCLES

Edith emerged from below into the wheelhouse to find Rachel bent over in pain.

The island was now just off the port side of the boat and only a few hundred feet away. She could see lush green vegetation covering the steep slopes emerging from the sea. Waves crashed against the jagged rocks as terns and seagulls floated on the wind. As the birds circled the island, their tweets and caws did nothing to drown out the pain and torment in Rachel's head.

"Rachel! You okay?!"

"No. I can't take this, anymore. The noise is unbearable."

"I don't hear anything. My gosh, your eyes are blood-red, and you're covered in sweat."

"I know. I'm going down below to take a shower."

"Sounds good. Let us know if you need anything."

"I will. Christin was on the forward deck sunbathing, but I think she moved to the aft deck."

"I see her through the window. She's out there on the

cargo hold hatch cover with her head on a pile of ropes, jamming away to her tunes."

Rachel wearily crossed over to the crew area. She stripped off her outer garments and proceeded to peel away the inner layers that had now become firmly stuck to her body from the sweat. She reached into the tiny shower closet, turned on the water and let it run until it was hot. She entered the tight shower and let the water wash over her back for a moment before she turned the shutoff valve on the showerhead to a trickle to conserve water. She began to think to herself, *How in the hell do Edith and Christin both fit in here at the same time?*

She lathered her body to remove the hours of sweat accumulation that had built up on her skin, smelling the bar of Irish Spring helped to soothe her agony a bit. She worked methodically to wash every nook and cranny before turning the valve back on and releasing their precious freshwater reserves to rinse away the soapy residue while also rinsing away some of the stresses of the day. She looked down at the bubbles circling down the drain and allowed the water to stream over her pounding head, letting it run through her hair and into her ears. As soon as the water entered her ear canal, the pain released its grip and the obnoxious tones subsided into a melodic song.

Rachel's eyes sprang open before she finished rinsing and she immediately felt the sting of the soap as it blinded her and sent her into spasms of blinking as her eyes teared up. She could hear the song as plain as if she were wearing headphones and listening to the radio. The soft lilting tones of a women's chorus poured into her water-filled ears as she plunged her head back under the water and finished rinsing off. Rachel shut off the water as the aria commenced and drew back the curtain to grab a towel. She frantically drew the droplets of water from her skin and ears.

Rachel stopped dead in her motions as if holding a pose. Christin was standing there watching the scene unfold. "Hey, girl, with gams like that, how are you still single?"

"Christin! Do you hear anything?"

"Nope, just admiring the view."

"I'm serious! The noise has been tormenting me again for the last several hours since the island came into view. I got into the shower and when I got water in my ears, the noise was replaced by a beautiful chorus of women's voices and the pain stopped. Now that I've dried my ears, the song and pains are gone."

"Really!? That's weird even for you." Christin said with a comical smirk.

"I'm not kidding. If it had gone on much longer, I would have taken a flare gun to my head and ended it all."

"I haven't heard anything except my Bob Marley and Jimmy Buffett tunes."

"Lucky you. I just wish I knew what was causing it."

Rachel finished toweling off and turned around to place the towel back on the towel bar when she felt an abrupt stinging pain in her left butt cheek, followed by a loud cracking sound. She spun around to see Christin smiling broadly back at her.

"I told you I would get you back."

"You bitch! I wasn't ready and my skin was still wet."

"Neither was I. Get dressed and let's go see how Edith's doing."

Rachel grabbed a clean pair of shorts and a tank top. She threw them on with a pair of flip flops and the two headed to the wheelhouse.

Rachel peered over the instruments as she entered the cabin. "What are you doing, Edith?"

"About ten knots in circles around the island. I wanted to see if I could spot a cave or somewhere to hide some treasure."

Rachel replied, "Really? With all the people that have come to this island before us looking for treasure and not finding it? Do you really think it will be that easy?"

"No, but I thought it might be a good idea to see how the island is laid out, so you don't need to be a bitch about it."

"Sorry. This awful ringing has taken a lot out of me and worn on my nerves."

"I know. Are you feeling any better?"

"Yes, actually I am. I got into the shower and when I got water in my ears the noise stopped and so did the pain."

"That's weird, even for you, Rach."

Christin said, "Hey, that's my line and I already used it. Find your own insult to use on her."

"Dang, are we a little touchy?" Edith snipped back.

"I'm just giving you a hard time. Get over it."

Rachel interrupted the spat. "Since we are trying to determine our next steps, let's continue to circle the island and see what we can learn before it gets too dark. You keep the helm; I'm going out on deck with the glasses and see if I can spot anything of interest. I just wish we knew what to do now that we're here."

"I'd like to go for a quick swim if we have a few minutes. It is hotter than the blazes of hell out here," Christin said.

"Okay. Edith, pull the throttles back and let's take a quick dip."

"Aye, aye, Cap'n. That's the most sensible thing I have heard all day. Throttles are dead and we are all stop."

Christin ran out on deck and was heading for the water when Rachel yelled out, "Hey! Stop! You don't know what it looks like under there. I don't want you getting hurt jumping in on a bloom of jellyfish or worse."

Christin came to a stop just short of losing her balance and tumbling overboard. "Okay, give me the underwater viewer and I'll take a quick look."

The viewer wasn't a complex or expensive piece of equipment; it was a simple device that gave Christin a clear view of what was below them in the water. Christin grabbed the viewer from Rachel and pulled the two covers off. She lay at the edge of the deck near a narrow access opening and leaned over the side. She placed the end with the clear panel down into the water and looked through it from above as she hung precariously from her waist.

"OH, JESUS CHRIST!"

"What is it?!" Rachel exclaimed as she headed over to where Christin was perched.

"Sharks! A shit-ton of sharks! All kinds! Hundreds, if not thousands of them!"

"Funny, Christin. Really funny."

Edith was also heading toward Christin after leaving the wheelhouse and hearing the conversation. "I turned on the hover control to keep us in place. Not sure how well it will work this close to the island and in these waves. It never seems to do much when we use it. I think I built it too small for a vessel of this size, but it isn't bad for being a bunch of scrap parts."

Rachel turned to Edith. "Come over here and let's see what Christin is going on about, then get your ass back in there before the waves put us into the rocks."

Rachel and Edith leaned over on either side of Christin and peered down through the viewer.

"Damn! You wanna go swimming in that?!" Edith inquired.

"Not anymore. I don't want to be chum for those bad boys."

"I don't think any of us would be much of an appetizer for those monsters," Rachel stated as her voice quivered.

"Okay, so swimming is out of the picture. What do you want to do now?" Edith inquired of Rachel.

"Let's go back to 'Plan A' and circle the island once more before dark."

"Alright, I'm going back to the helm; you two enjoy yourselves sightseeing through the binoculars."

Edith brought the engines back to life with a roar and they resumed their counterclockwise trek around the jagged coast.

Several hours passed before they finally completed their first circumnavigation of the island and the sun was setting. The sky was ablaze with reds, blues, oranges, yellows, purples, and grays. It became dotted with tiny white specks as the stars began to emerge from their slumber, creating a spectacular display.

When the sun had completely set except for a thin band of twilight, Christin went down below to cook dinner. The smell of butter, creole seasoning, and fish permeated the air followed by the sweet intoxicating smells of cinnamon plantains in bourbon sauce.

Rachel was at the helm and Edith was watching the instrument panel as they made another loop around the island in the dark to see if things looked any different. Christin entered the wheelhouse with three piping hot plates of food and served each of her fellow crew members a meal fit for a king.

"Girl, are you trying to make me fat with all the gourmet

cooking you're doing?" Edith ate half of a cheese and guaca-mole-filled tortilla in one bite.

"Hell, you could do with a bit of softening. When we snuggle, I like to feel a few curves now and then. Not that I don't like your muscles and cut figure, mind you, but sometimes a little love handle is nice to grab, too."

"I think we are all getting a little soft since we aren't working our asses off hauling nets and gutting fish."

"When was the last time you hauled a net, Rach? Shit, Christin and I do all the hard stuff."

"Yeah, yeah, I hear you. But I don't eat like you two do, either."

"Christin, this is great!" Edith kissed her cheek.

"Well, don't worry, I'm not done yet, I have this bottle of rum I've been holding back to celebrate our arrival."

Edith reached out her hand. "You sly minx! Gimme a snort of that." She grabbed the bottle and gulped down a healthy portion before handing it off to Rachel.

"Just a small one. I'm driving."

Rachel took a quick pull off the bottle and handed it to Christin, who finally got to whet her palate on the fine Panamanian liquor. "Boy, when they say spiced rum, they mean it. That's great. I'm going to go grab a cola and do it up right. Anyone else want one?" Christin asked as she disappeared back into the galley without waiting for a response.

The three ate and drank and made light of the evening as they basked in the glow of the electric aura being emitted from the instruments.

After a while, Christin retired with the dirty dishes and empty bottles. "I'm going to clean these up and head to bed. Wake me up for my shift."

"We will. Sleep tight. Gimme a quick kiss before you go down."

Christin gave Edith a quick peck on the lips and slipped away silently.

"It is so nice to be able to finally sit here without all the noise and pain banging in my head," Rachel commented.

"What Christin and I dealt with was bad enough. I can't imagine what you were going through. Do you think it will come back again?"

"God, I hope not. If it does, I don't know what I will do. Right now, I am just worried about figuring out what to do next. I don't want to be out here killing time, doing endless circles around this island. That sure won't get us anywhere. Do you have any ideas?"

Edith looked up from the instrument panel and cast a brief glance at Rachel. Her face was lit with a red-tinged glow from below. It was reminiscent of her days as a child camping in the Adirondacks and telling ghost stories around a campfire with a flashlight under her chin. "I'm not the one that is being led on this journey. I'm just a passenger on your flight of fancy. Just sit back, relax, and let things happen like they are supposed to. Surrender yourself to the quest for once and go at it without planning every step. You said you were going to take things as they come on this trip, just like when we are fishing, but you haven't done that. You've tried to control every move and plan every action. You are so OCD about planning things that you can't go to the grocery store without first visiting an expedition outfitter. Someone is guiding you, so just let them. It's worked up to this point when you've let it."

Rachel shrugged her shoulders. "I guess you're right. I just hate the unknown. The unknown has killed too many of our friends and I don't want us to be next."

"Be that as it may, the unknown is where excitement and wonder exist. Every time we leave port we head into the unknown. Knowing where you are on a map doesn't mean shit. Without the unknown, we could never experience anything new, and life would be pretty dull. Hell, fishing is nothing but unknown. You think you know where they'll be, and you plan your routes based on your best guess. You have been lucky so many times that you take the unknown for granted. Every time we cast a net it's a crapshoot. You know I'm right. Granted, you have the knack, but it could come to an end at any time and your luck could run out."

"I know you're right. I do take my luck for granted. When we head out, it's like someone is taking me by the hand and guiding me to the fish. I can't explain it, but that is what it feels like. Sometimes it scares the shit out of me when the feelings become so strong and I want to resist them, but I can't. So many times, I don't feel like I even have control of my own body when we are heading out. Do you know what I mean?"

"Not at all, you freaky witch. You're telling me that all this time someone has cast a spell on you?"

"It sure feels that way. Maybe there is a voodoo priestess out there making me do the things I do. Maybe, it's Odin's hand guiding me, or maybe it is the will of my father. I can't explain it, but it seems to work for us."

"Well, there you have it. Treat this like another fishing trip and let it happen like it always does. You don't need to be in control every minute."

"That's funny. Most times I would just like to be in control for a single minute." Rachel caressed her pendant, hanging between her breasts. She released a soft sigh. Retrieving the weighty geode, she knew every inch of it by now. Her fingers investigated the crevices and crystalline peaks contained within the central cavity. It gave her energy and brought her calm in times when she needed to focus. It was almost as if it spoke to her on a mystical level; like it knew and understood her needs and desires.

"Okay. Well, I'm heading below to catch a few winks before I have to take the watch again."

"Good night, Edith. See you in a few hours. Thank you for all you do. I love you both and I don't know anyone else crazy enough to follow me all the way out here on a quest for treasure and pirate booty."

"Shit, this is vacation. We aren't fishing, and I am getting one hell of a tan down here in the tropics. This isn't crazy, it's relaxing… it is a bit crazy."

"Get out of here and let me do my job."

"Later."

Edith slid quietly from the wheelhouse, leaving Rachel to her own whims and thoughts.

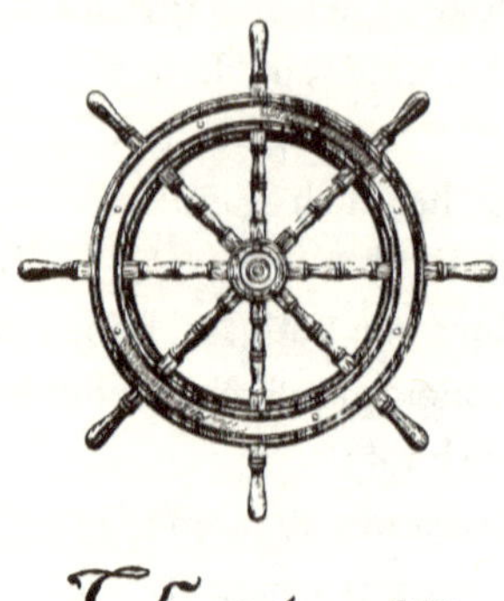

Chapter 17

THE DEAFENING SILENCE OF NIGHT

In silence, Rachel sat in her chair at the helm as the moonlight danced off the waves, making the sea move in a rhythmic motion similar to figures on a dance floor enjoying a slow waltz. The only companion around was the sea itself.

Rachel relished these moments since they were so few and far between when fishing. She looked at the charts of the island under the dim glow of the red cabin lights. By now, she knew every line on that chart. Every inlet, cove, peninsula, hill, and shoal.

The dim lights and lack of sleep played tricks on her eyes and made it difficult to focus. She folded the brittle paper and set it aside as the waves moved the boat ever so slowly, rocking gently back and forth. When she sat in her chair she felt as secure as a baby in a bassinette. Many times, she was lulled into a trance or momentary sleep by the therapeutic rocking. Oftentimes, the line between a dream and reality became so blurred; she would have to pinch herself to make sure she was truly awake.

As the minutes passed, she drifted ever closer to that trance-like state. The engines droned their familiar sound, causing her eyes to become heavier until they finally shut completely.

Rachel had been nodding off for only a few seconds when she was yanked from her slumber by something familiar, yet seemingly out of place. An overwhelming smell of vanilla attacked her senses with a forceful vengeance akin to ammonia. She choked and coughed for a moment and wiped the drool from her chin. She blinked her eyes and as fast as the smell had overwhelmed her, it was gone without a trace.

She breathed in quickly and heavily as her heart heaved in her chest. The air was thick and she was sweating profusely. As she regained her composure and tried to piece together the startling event, she thought, *Okay, you have my attention. What do I need to do?* The console lights flickered as if in response to her silent query.

Rachel rose from her seat and attempted to shake the fog from her brain. She felt as if the world was weighing down on her. Even the pendant around her neck took on an unfamiliar weight as the chain dug into her skin. She undid the clasp and removed it to help relieve her distress. She hung it on a screw protruding above the cabin's main window. It dangled and danced with every movement of the ship as if trying to hypnotize her.

Once again Rachel slid back into her chair and became a slave to the silence. She watched the pendant swing in the moonlight. It wasn't long before its hypnotic rhythm placed her once again into a trance. Her eyes closed under the strain of exhaustion and the weight of her burdens. Barely a moment had passed when she was once again wrenched from her sleep. This time she could have sworn that a voice spoke to her. Softly, she heard the words, "I am here with you."

Two such occurrences were not normal in any circum-stances. Could it be that she was dreaming? Could the exhaus-tion be causing her to hallucinate or imagine such oddities? Could the headaches and strange sounds be inducing mind-al-tering phenomena?

Her heart continued to race once again as she whispered into the silence, "I know you are here. I need you now more than ever. I'm ready for you to guide me."

Rachel knew she would have a hard time going back to sleep now, so with a renewed vigor she once again unfolded the old chart and laid it out on the console under the dim red lights. She studied it ever so intently. She was determined to find what it was she was overlooking.

With a magnifier, she searched every inch of the parch-ment for the most minute details that could guide her. After about twenty minutes, she felt her eyes once again weighing down. This time she did not fight the effects. She leaned back comfortably in her chair and closed her eyes. Nothing hap-pened. She could not sleep. She opened her eyes and noticed the pendant fluidly swinging back and forth in front of her. This time no trance overtook her body and mind.

Rachel repositioned herself in her chair and began to fid-dle with some of the many knobs and switches that didn't do anything of special significance. She occasionally glanced out the window in the direction of the coastline. Periodically, the waves lapping on the rocks would catch the moonlight just right and she could see a faint outline of what existed just be-yond the limits of her night vision.

The seconds turned to minutes and the minutes began to feel like eons as they languidly passed. Rachel turned her gaze to the chart again as she thought to herself, *I'm trying too hard. These things are happening because I want them to. They aren't real and I am driving myself insane. The best thing we can do is give up and go home. I'm not the captain of a ship of fools.*

Suddenly, she heard the words: "You belong here with me. Don't doubt yourself."

Rachel's heart leaped from her chest and she began to shake. This time she knew it was real. She was completely awake. She wasn't dreaming and there was no one in the cabin with her.

Once again, after a short time passed and she had calmed herself, she began to question her mental state and if what she had experienced was real. She felt a lump in the pit of her stomach as her hands continued to shake. Rachel felt no fear, but she worried that the quest was taking too much of a toll on her and the crew. She worried that it had been a big mistake and she was following a fool's quest.

The ship continued to pitch and roll with a regularity that would challenge the accuracy of the finest Swiss timepiece or metronome. She watched the moonlight dance on the waves as they tilted left and right with every roll of the ship. In an instant, she realized something was wrong, but she could not identify exactly what it was. She scanned the cabin space to determine the cause of her sudden anxiety, but she could find nothing out of place.

Rachel sat back in her chair yet again and stared straight ahead into the dark abyss of night. Then it struck her, and she was overcome with a horror that she had never experienced before. Her every sense was heightened and it felt as if a million ants were crawling over her body. Her chest burned with an intense pain as every one of her fear responses reacted at once. Her stomach quivered and she felt as if she was going to throw up as she glared at a seemingly impossible sight.

In front of her hung the pendant she had treasured since she had discovered it in the old box at Gwen's house. This time, the pendant that was swinging so fluidly only a minute earlier was now frozen before her in a stationary fixation. The boat continued to pitch and roll, but the pendant did not move. It hung on its chain with an uncharacteristic heaviness like it was being held in position by a tremendous force. Rachel reached out her hand to touch the pendant and just as she neared it, everything went black.

Rachel froze in fear as a complete and unwavering silence overcame the vessel. The instruments were dead, the engines and various other equipment no longer droned their songs. Not even the rigging produced any sound. The only sounds she heard were the ocean waves crashing on the shore and a faint choral melody being carried on the night air from an indeterminate place.

As Rachel sat in the dark and her eyes adjusted to the dimness of the environment into which she had been plunged, the faint smell of vanilla once again invaded her consciousness. She drew her hand back from the pendant and continued to peer into the space where it was frozen.

All she could think was, *We are going to lose the boat on the rocks if we don't get things running again. Those girls need to wake up, quick.*

None of the emergency lighting was on and the ship was engulfed in utter blackness. The emergency batteries did not kick in and the auxiliary generator did not turn over. Nothing was as it should be. They were truly dead in the water and at the mercy of the sea.

A voice cut through the silence like a fine sword through an unarmored foe. "Trust me. Look down."

Now with Rachel's eyes adjusted to the darkness, she could see a faint glow appear on the chart she had studied so many times. The glow matched the shape of the island perfectly along every contour. It was apparent that the moonlight was shining through her motionless pendant and casting a glow on the chart.

In the faint glow, new details began to emerge. Within the contours, she could see a small black dot near the coastline where a large hill met the sea. From that location, a fine, almost imperceptible line, ran along a route to the coast. At the island's edge was a rectangular-shaped symbol with a black spot to the left of it. Above the rectangle was a series of squiggles that appeared to represent waves.

Rachel grabbed a charting pen and began to quickly trace the faint apparitions onto the chart. As her pen made the last stroke, the image faded, and the pendant began to swing freely once more.

Rachel was still slumped over the chart with the pen in her hand when the engines suddenly roared to life. Next, all her instruments awoke in the same state they were in before the darkness and silence struck. They flooded the cabin with the eerie glow of electric light. She was blinded by the sudden brightness of the lights in the cabin even though everything was dimmed and rigged for night-time operation. She slid back into position in her chair and picked up the chart to study her tracings. It appeared that she finally had the key to their success. This was no longer a fool's quest.

Rachel studied the chart for several minutes before she realized that everything was back to normal and her crew had never woken to deal with the failures. She gently refolded the old parchment with great care as if it were made from the most delicate gossamer fabric.

Rachel sat motionless in the darkness for nearly another forty-five minutes before Edith arrived to relieve her. She contemplated what she had experienced and realized that the manifestations were real. She was confident that she wasn't losing her mind and she realized that all this time she had been guided through life by a paranormal force. She finally understood that this quest was meant for her alone and it was her duty to complete it.

Edith chugged a big mouthful of coffee before she spoke. "Morning, Rachel. Anything going on?"

"Nope. It's been quiet all night," she stated with a mischievous grin.

"What's that funny little smirk all about?"

"Awe, nothing. I do have a plan though. I'll share it with you both in the morning. Right now, I need some sleep. See you in a few hours."

"Okay. Sleep well. When you go below, check Christin's alarm clock and make sure the alarm is turned on. I don't need her sandbagging me on the watch relief."

"I'll do that. Have a good morning."

Rachel slid below and disappeared into the dark muffled silence of the crew area. This time she did not fear the darkness or the silence. She looked forward to the dreams to come and what they might reveal to her.

Chapter 18

VISIT COCOS AND MEET
THE FRIENDLY LOCALS

"Hey! Get up here, quick! We've got company!" Edith shouted with an urgency uncharacteristic of her laid-back and unwavering demeanor. Rachel burst into the wheelhouse half asleep with a look of fear stretching across her face. As she entered the cabin, she tripped over the threshold of the hatch and fell to her knees. She rolled to her side, reeling in terrible pain, "Dammit! That hurts like hell." She breathed heavily through her clenched teeth as she grasped her right knee and pulled it to her chest.

As Christin stepped through the open hatch she stumbled over Rachel's extended left leg causing her to lurch into the compartment, sending her tumbling face-first toward the command console. She stopped just short of hitting it by gripping the back of the captain's chair at the last second. This action spun her sideways and she nearly hit the side of her head on the rounded corner of the console, "Shit, Rachel! Do you have to camp out in front of the hatch like that? You coulda killed me!"

"Oh, shut up! I'm not doing much better here. I'm just hoping I didn't break anything." Rachel glared at Christin in disdain.

Christin wrestled her muscular frame back to her feet. "What's so fucking important anyway?!"

Edith barely paid any attention to the scene of carnage that lay around her. She had her eyes focused on a dark silhouette approaching them from around the island. A faint sound of sirens and flashing lights were all she needed to know they were in trouble. "It looks like the local Mounties are paying us a visit. You girls need to be on your best behavior. Rachel, you want the chair?"

"Yeah, I'll take it if you can help me up off the floor. Edith, go out on the bow and greet them so they know we aren't a threat. I wonder why they didn't call first if they planned to come to breakfast?"

Edith helped Rachel to her feet and sat her in the chair with a powerful thrust from her muscular arms. "There you go. Christin, you okay?"

"I'm fine, except for this massive lump on my head."

"You'll be okay. We'll put some ice on it when we finish taking care of this situation."

"Yeah, yeah. Just get out there. I'll be there in a minute."

Edith emerged from the wheelhouse noting the two official-looking watercraft. She stood next to the cabin on the port side and waved at the first approaching vessel. All she could think was, *I sure hope they're friendly.*

A few seconds later they could hear a woman's voice over the PA speakers from the first boat: "*Barco pesquero. Prepararse para ser abordado.*" The message was repeated three times as her boat pulled alongside *Lady Destiny* and a crewman cast a line over to Edith. She tied the line to the closest cleat and tried to manage the friendliest smile she could, saying, "Hello. Welcome aboard."

The first person across was an attractive Costa Rican woman about thirty-five years of age wearing a beige shirt and green shorts. It was obvious that she was a member of the Costa Rican Park Rangers that patrolled the island and provided security for the protected national park. Her hair was long, black, and shined brilliantly in the morning sun. She kept it pulled back in a ponytail which fully exposed her blemish-free face. Edith reached out her hand and helped her aboard.

The ranger carried a fully loaded Uzi over her right shoulder and an extra clip on her belt next to a grossly oversized radio. Her face did not show the same friendliness that Edith was trying to convey.

Edith next helped a younger, also well-armed, male ranger aboard. Edith smiled and nodded to him, but he did not return or even acknowledge the gesture. He appeared to be about twenty-five years old with a thin build. His legs were scarred from what looked like repeated cuts of some sort. She assumed that he had spent his younger years working in the cane fields which had sliced his legs, leaving the deep scars. His grip was strong, and Edith returned the strength in kind as she steadied him on his passage between the vessels.

Edith turned to the female ranger since she assumed it was her voice they had heard booming before. "How may I help you?"

"You speak English. That is good, so do I."

Edith responded with a small nod of understanding.

"Tell the rest of your crew to join us on deck. How many are aboard?"

"Three," Edith responded, as she turned to gesture to

Rachel and Christin through the window to come down and join them.

Rachel limped out from the cabin with Christin in tow.

"What is wrong with them? Where are your men?"

"They fell over each other when they were coming up from below to meet you. We are also the entire crew," Edith responded with a cocky smirk.

"You are a fishing vessel with only a crew of three women? I do not believe you. Ramone! Search the vessel." The thin male ranger made his way past the three women as if they didn't exist and proceeded to search every corner of the ship. At the same time, another ranger emerged on the opposite vessel with his weapon drawn, strategically pointed so that no matter what happened he would hit at least one of the three women undergoing questioning.

"Carlos, keep an eye on these three and watch for others. I don't want any surprises."

The ranger motioned for them to move to a more open area at the back of the boat, and they all eagerly complied.

"Sit on that locker and keep your hands in front of you where I can see them." The three sat in unison and folded their hands in their laps stiffly.

Rachel piped in. "Did we do something wrong? I don't understand what this is about."

"I will speak with you in a minute, once I know everything is secure and there will be no distractions or unexpected interruptions."

The four remained on the deck for about another ten minutes in silence, except for the occasional crack of the radio on the ranger's boat. Finally, the thin ranger named Ramone emerged from the *Lady Destiny* and motioned to the female ranger with a silent nod while waving to the second ranger on the other vessel that all was clear. He then stepped back and steadied himself against a storage locker.

At that moment the female ranger acknowledged the gesture and turned her attention toward Edith and said, "So, what is a fishing vessel with a three-woman crew doing here?"

Rachel spoke up. "I am the captain of this vessel and I would appreciate it if you would direct your questions to me, if that is agreeable."

"You are the captain?" the ranger countered derisively with a hateful gaze. "Then answer me. What are you doing here?!"

"We are here on vacation to do some diving and enjoy the island. I have a permit to anchor."

"Let me see your permit."

"I'll get it as long as I can get some bottled water, if that's acceptable," Christin interrupted abruptly.

"That is fine. My ranger, Lieutenant Diaz, will escort you below."

Ramone stood up straight and began walking toward Christin. "Okay, Ramone. Let's go."

Lieutenant Diaz frowned in disgust at the flippant air of disrespect Christin was exuding toward him.

The two were gone about two minutes before they emerged with Christin carrying a few bottles of water and a file folder under her arm. The female ranger took the folder and spent an additional ten minutes reading through the documents it contained. "Everything seems to be in order. Why did you not contact the ranger station when you arrived as instructed on the permit?"

"We did. Many times, but we never got a response," Rachel replied.

"We heard several calls at the station from your trawler and we responded to them, but we received no responses in return. Over the last few hours, we have been observing you as your ship circled the island. We again attempted to make contact, but still, you did not respond.

"We consider these actions hostile and the sign of a poacher or someone who should not be here. Therefore, we were forced to intercept your vessel and investigate," the ranger admonished sternly. "I take it from the paperwork that you are Rachel, and these are your crew members, Christin and Edith?" Both women introduced themselves to the ranger.

"Very well, Captain. You will escort me to your wheelhouse and we will test your radio."

"Yes, ma'am. Follow me." The ranger followed Rachel as she limped back into the wheelhouse and plopped down in her chair.

"I see you are tuned to the proper frequency. Hand me the mic."

Rachel passed the mic to the ranger as she leaned out of the window to view the patrol boat below. "Cocos Base, this is Ranger One Patrol. Acknowledge." The ranger paused several seconds and repeated the message. Still no response. She waved to the ranger on the boat below. The other ranger, Carlos, gestured that he could not hear the calls.

"It appears that you have a defective radio. Do you have a backup radio onboard?"

"Yes, we do. It's over there." Rachel gestured toward a radio on the auxiliary console.

The ranger handed the mic back to Rachel. As she hung it back in place, she noticed that the wires near the plug on the radio were exposed and broken. "It looks like my chair has been rubbing against the cord and may have broken the wire. I have a spare mic if you want to try that."

"Get it," the ranger directed.

Rachel reached into a drawer and pulled out a shiny new microphone to replace the old one. Immediately the speaker in the microphone sprang to life with the sounds of squelch-filled conversation. "I guess that was the problem. I should have switched it over to the overhead speakers, but we've been taking shifts sleeping and I didn't want to wake the crew."

"It seems we have resolved our dilemma. Join me back on deck."

Rachel followed the ranger out on deck as she motioned for the other rangers to lower their weapons and gave the all-clear. Rachel limped back to the locker and resumed her position between Edith and Christin. "Excuse me, officer, I know that the gentleman over there is Ramone and the guy perched on your boat is Carlos, but we don't know your name."

"Yes, Lieutenant Diaz is my second-in-command and Ensign Carlos Crespo is my junior officer in training. I am Major Maria Aroza of the Costa Rican Park Rangers. This is my duty station, and these men are part of my crew." Rachel discovered she could listen to Maria's softly-accented voice all day.

"Well, welcome aboard the *Lady Destiny*, Major. What else can we do for you?"

Major Aroza cracked a tight little smile and her demeanor seemed to shift as she spoke. "We can start by discussing your visit to this beautiful island paradise of ours. It seems odd to have such a vessel visit our island unless you intend to plunder our resources. I also have never seen a vessel of this size or type, commanded and crewed by a team of only three women."

"Yes, we are an odd crew, but I trust these women with my life. They are the best fishing crew around. As you can see, we do not have any nets on board and we only have two fishing poles to provide a little fresh fish on our trip. We came here after years of fishing to finally take a well-deserved vacation. We just want to relax on a tropical island and do some diving."

"I see. Where is your diving flag then?"

"Under my butt in this locker with our dive gear," Rachel replied with a smile.

"I believe you, but I still find it hard to believe that this vessel could be run by such a meager crew."

"Major Aroza, these women have been by my side for years and I love them dearly. They work hard and serve me well. I have the utmost respect for them and even when we fight like wild cats, we still care about each other. They would fight to the death for me and I would do the same for them. They are my family and my business partners. I wouldn't have anyone else with me on this trip. I owe my life and my livelihood to these two women. We may be a small crew on a big boat, but don't underestimate our spirit or abilities. As you can see, Edith has made many modifications to this vessel which enables us to fish with minimal crew. We hire a few local deckhands when we need additional assistance. This saves money because I do not have to pay for a full permanent crew all year. We don't always catch the most, but we give the other boats a hefty amount of competition."

"I can respect that, but you are a long way from home in a place you have never been without any clue about what to expect. The sheer uncertainty alone is enough to scare most people into quitting such a trek and returning home."

"Not us! We have been through hell together and we still have a long way to go before we get to the other side," Edith interrupted.

"I do not mean any disrespect by my comments. I am just perplexed by the oddity of it all. How long do you plan to stay around the island?"

"We have been planning this trip for a long time and I haven't had a good vacation in years. I would like to stay up to three weeks if the food and fuel hold out and the boss doesn't decide to go back to work early," Christin stated with a toothy grin.

"Your permit allows you up to a maximum of seventeen days and that is all. If you are here longer than that, you will be required to file for an extension three days in advance of the expiration date. Failure to comply could result in you and your crew being arrested if you have not left the area by the prescribed time and date."

Rachel looked Major Aroza square in the eye. "We understand. We are not here to cause any trouble. We just want a little quiet time away from the rest of the world with the ability to enjoy a tropical paradise away from the cold of New England."

"That's all fine. Just remember that you are a visitor in a land governed by the Costa Rican government and you must abide by our rules. You may only anchor in designated areas to protect our reefs. If you wish to come ashore, you must get permission from the rangers and adhere to the allotted times and locations to protect the island from tourism damage. And, most importantly, if you choose to dive, be aware that you are in waters that team with sharks and other creatures that could kill you in seconds. I personally think you picked the wrong place to go diving and you should have planned better."

"We understand completely, and we will comply with your orders, Major. As for the diving part, we knew there would be sharks and we have dived with sharks many times. We just weren't expecting such dangerous varieties in such vast numbers," Rachel said sheepishly.

"I am satisfied with your answers and with the resolution to your radio issues. You are now welcomed visitors to our national park. Do not poach or endanger our inhabitants, above or below the water, or you will be subject to arrest and imprisonment. Give me your passports so I can stamp them."

Rachel handed the major their passports from the folder containing their permits and other documents. "We understand completely. May I ask you a question?"

"Sure. What would you like to know?"

"You speak English very well. I know most Costa Ricans speak English, but yours is impeccable."

"Ah, you noticed. I spent part of my life growing up in Southern California. I attended college at the University of California, Los Angeles. I graduated with a degree in marine biology."

"Wow, that's impressive. Christin and Edith have degrees as well. Edith has a master's in marine engineering and Christin has a degree in business."

"I would like to have a conversation with you all one day in a less formal setting. I am on rotation for the next twenty days, so just radio us if you would like to join us on the island. I can give you a brief tour of our home away from home and we can share time together with my team over a fine meal prepared just for you. I would like to learn more about your adventures and how you handle this vessel."

"Thank you, Major. We would love to do that," Edith said with a big smile.

The major handed their passports back. "Very well. I will see myself back to my patrol boat, and we will let you get back to your vacation. Keep your radio on and check in with us every couple of days so we know you are alright. If we do not hear from you every three days, we will send a patrol to check on you.

"Occasionally we have trouble with poachers and treasure hunters. We don't want you getting caught up in that or getting hurt. These waters can be dangerous if you find yourself in the crossfire."

Rachel felt a lump in the pit of her stomach as she stood and reached out a hand toward the major. "We will do our best to stay safe and we will check in as you request. Thank you for your time."

"You are welcome. Be safe."

"Thank you. Goodbye." The girls shouted in unison as the patrol boat fired up its engines and floated away, the second boat following. They all waved and when both patrol boats were a fair distance away, each woman let out a huge sigh of relief.

Edith commented first. "We know they don't take any crap and they hate poachers and treasure hunters."

"Luckily we are only one of those and they don't know it. I'm sure we will be watched. They will know our every move, especially if they don't have anyone else to watch. We will have to be extra cautious to not draw any suspicion as we explore," Rachel said as Christin nodded in agreement.

"I have never been this scared or excited in my life. I can't tell if I'm going to explode or puke."

"Dang, Christin, did you have to go there? You know I hate that word," Edith said with a grimace.

"Sorry. Maybe I should have said hurl? Puke is just so much easier and fun to say."

"Oh, that's sooo much better," Edith said.

"Yep, and I'm proud of it. No fear here. Let's get hunting," Christin replied after a long belch.

"Alright, you two. We are going to have to plan out all of our activities since they'll be watching all of our moves. They may even time our dives, so we'll have to make it look like everything is above-board. Right now, we need to find a location to start our search. We can only hope they won't expect three women to be here on a treasure-hunting expedition. It could work to our advantage."

"Rachel, you told me this morning when I relieved you that you had a plan and you would tell us about it in the morning. Seems like now is the time."

"Okay. Let's go inside and I'll show you what I have in mind."

"I'm glad you finally decided to include me in all this," Christin touted grumpily.

"Shit, we couldn't get you to wake up from your beauty sleep. From the looks of that lump, you are going to need a lot more. Hell, I'm beginning to think you're accident-prone."

"Ha, ha, very funny. I'm just fine. Now let's get down to it."

"Aye, aye, Cap'n Bligh!" Edith joked back.

They spent the remainder of the day studying the maps and planning their activities as Rachel recounted her experiences from the night before.

The *Destiny* crew made final checks on their dive equipment and selected a few locations that were not in any obvious vicinity to their final dive location. They prepared a fine meal of sea bass and a fresh fruit salad which they downed with a celebratory bottle of wine that Christin had hidden away in some dark and inconspicuous corner of the crew area. Rachel did the dishes as Christin took over the watch in the wheelhouse. Edith headed to bed first so she could relieve Christin at the end of her watch.

They settled into the night with a cool breeze blowing and the sound of waves lapping against the side. Occasionally the hypnotizing rhythm of the night was broken by the cackles, whistles, and screams of various seabirds passing their vessel as they foraged for their next meal in the dim moonlight.

Christin put her headphones on and kicked back in the captain's chair with a magazine she had read no less than a dozen times. It wasn't long before she settled into her familiar routine punctuated only by the occasional shooting star.

Chapter 19

THE TEST OF THE ANCIENT MARINER

The morning broke with a dazzling display of scarlets, oranges, blues, and the deepest purples imaginable. The colors danced and floated on the horizon as the sun prepared to enter the stage to welcome the new day. A soft breeze blew through the ship and over the crew; each delicate waft of air invigorated and refreshed the soul. It filled their lungs and gave them renewed energy. This was the first day of the next phase of an epic adventure.

Edith walked out on deck with a big mug of coffee and surveyed the seas around them. The swells were small, and the surface was remarkably calm. She brought the cup to her lips and took a big gulp of the bitter black elixir that helped to awaken her senses and spring her into conscientiousness. At the same time, she took her free hand and wiped the sleep from her eyes. She arched her back as if presenting her ample breasts to the sun god, Ra, for inspection through her thin shirt. Her back cracked as she twisted slightly from right to left. She finally arched forward and then back to vertical.

She viewed the sunrise once more as the sun began to peep over the horizon. Edith cocked her head from side to side and her neck cracked out a familiar tune. She smiled and took a seat on one of the deck boxes lashed to the deck. The growing intensity of the sun washed over her as she absorbed its energy.

Edith thought to herself, *This is going to be a good day. I can feel it.* She became aware of a presence behind her and felt a pair of hands reach into the sides of her loose-fitting T-shirt and cup her breasts.

"Good morning, Christin," she whispered with a grin.

"Good morning, love." Christin leaned over, and they shared a long kiss. "It sure is a beautiful morning and you look so good in the glow of the morning sun. I understand now why photographers call this the 'Magic Hour.'"

"You look beautiful, too," Edith replied. "This is the big day. The day we finally get to begin the search for treasure."

"I don't care if we ever find anything. As far as I'm concerned, the trip has been one of the greatest experiences of my life and I will cherish it forever."

"I agree. Well, I guess we should check in with Rachel and get the plan." Edith stood and the couple turned toward the wheelhouse.

Rachel was sitting at the helm console, poring over a few charts. Without looking up, she greeted her crew. "Good morning, ladies. You ready to get wet?"

Christin chirped, "Hell, I woke up wet, but Edith wasn't around to take care of it."

"Ha, ha. You know what I mean," Rachel replied with an annoyed stare.

"Just kidding. Dang, get the stick out and start having a little fun."

"Sorry, I have had a little headache all morning and my ears are ringing."

Edith took another sip of her coffee before adding to the discussion. "I don't know if you've noticed, but we are being watched this morning."

"How do you know?" Rachel inquired.

"As the sun was rising this morning, I could see the glint of binoculars from the island. I don't think they were watching the sunrise with the same vigor that I was. I suggest that we do a test dive this morning in another location. That should throw them off our trail for a little while and it will ensure that our gear is in good order before we commit to something more serious."

"I agree. I was thinking the same thing," Rachel replied. "I have picked out an area off the northeast corner of the island, not too far from the ranger station. That way they will have an easy time watching us. How do you feel about the sharks?"

Edith revealed a slight grin. "I've dived with sharks many times and I've never had any trouble. I know how to handle them."

"You may know how to handle a couple of them at once, but these waters are teeming with thousands of them," Christin said with a tone of grave concern.

"I know, honey. This isn't any different. It's like being the only girl at a frat party. Be proud, confident, and carry a big stick. If they get too pushy, push back. They don't like their delicate noses punched. Just like frat boys."

"Either way, we all need to be careful and aware of everything around us at all times. We will dive in pairs and take extended decompression periods between dives. I'm afraid we may take on a lot more nitrogen if we get nervous during the dive and breathe heavier. The last thing we need or want out here is someone to get a case of the bends," Rachel said.

"Sounds like a plan to me," Edith responded anxiously.

"Come on, Christin. We're going first. Let's get the gear ready and get wet."

"Okay, but this is my first-time diving with sharks in the wild. Closest I've been to them before was when I visited Disney World and snorkeled in the shark reef lagoon. Those were just a few small lemon, sand, and leopard sharks, so it was no big deal."

"It'll be a piece of cake; just follow my lead. I also have some current stimulators that send out a small charge around them that we won't feel but should help keep the sharks from coming in too close." Edith set her empty cup down and exited the cabin with Christin in tow.

After retrieving the anchor, Rachel shoved the throttles forward and the engines once more roared and wheezed to life with a belch of black from the twin stacks behind the main cabin. The twin bronze screws began pushing the hulking vessel through the mild surf toward the spot she had chosen.

As they approached the dive site, Edith and Christin were already geared up and completing the final checks on their equipment. Rachel throttled back the engines to a barely noticeable drone. She leaned out the window. "You two about ready?"

"Yep, ready as we can be," Edith responded with excited vigor.

"I guess I'm ready, but I gotta say, this scares the hell out of me. I think I'm going to hurl," Christin replied with apprehension in her voice.

"Oh, you'll be okay. Just stay close to me and you'll do fine. We'll either be part of the party or we'll be the hors d'oeuvres. One way or another, this will be an experience of a lifetime. I'll take the camera, so you can hold the strike stick, if that will make you feel better."

"That would be better," Christin stated as her hands trembled uncontrollably.

"Just remember that it is just a stick. Tap it on their nose if they come too close and they should turn away. If they are a bit more aggressive, push the button and when the stick makes contact, they will get a little jolt of electricity. If we run into a real badass that won't take a subtle hint and tries to attack us, use the other end and jam it into them. It will discharge a 12-gauge shotgun shell into them. But remember that the shotgun shell is a last resort. If we kill a shark, we'll end up in jail."

"Okay, I got it. Let's just get this done."

"Alright, masks down. Pressure looks good. Regulators in." Edith winked at Christin as the two rolled back and over the side into the shark-infested waters.

At first, the sharks scattered from the splash. The two foreign figures hung nearly motionless and peered down into the strange translucent abyss. Most of the sharks were well below them except for a few of the larger and more curious specimens. Edith looked at Christin and gave her an 'OK" sign. Christin responded in a like manner, but the fear was evident in her eyes.

The two descended slowly toward an area of greater activity near the walls of the reef extending down from the island. They could see a multitude of sharks swimming in what seemed to be a well-choreographed pattern. They weaved in and out, passing each other ever so closely but never touching. Edith and Christin slid into the dance and hovered, nearly motionless back-to-back as the performance carried on around them. Occasionally, one performer would miss its mark and pass within inches of them. Edith would reach out a hand and touch them and they would immediately turn away.

Christin clutched the strike stick with every ounce of her strength as if losing it would mean doom and certain death. Her knuckles ached and her forearms throbbed from the intensity of her grasp. Her glare was wide and intense as she watched each creature approach and at the last instant turn away. They appeared to be studying her as much as she was studying them. Those that came too close were hit with an abrupt jab from the stick to the side of their nose and they immediately changed course.

Edith was absorbing every moment of the experience as she grinned under her regulator mouthpiece. Her heart beat wildly, and she could feel every pulse as her blood pumped through her body. Her breaths were slow and measured as she gazed with childish delight as a large hammerhead slid up next to her from behind her right shoulder, momentarily startling her. She reached out a hand and caressed its side. She slid her hand down to its tail as it glided effortlessly past. The creature was nearly twelve feet in length. It never quivered or showed any sign to acknowledge her contact. As its tail slid past her, she could feel its power as it gave a brisk flick that sent a rush of current past them. The current caused the couple to drift several feet apart and for a moment they were separated.

Christin sensed the distance and turned toward Edith just in time to see a large tiger shark pass between them. Her chest pounded and she felt nauseated. She could only catch a glimpse of Edith as its massive body slid silently between them. She was caught in an internal battle. She could not decide if she should push the shark away, hit it with the stick, give it a jolt, or unload on it completely. In a split second, she caught herself losing control and went through the possibilities and ramifications in her head. Pushing it away might cause it to feel threatened and make it turn. Hitting it with a stick or jolt of electricity could do the same or possibly make it angry. Unloading on it completely could not be justified even in the throes of her worst fear since it wasn't doing anything to indicate it had hostile intentions.

Instead, Christin reached out her hand and allowed her fingertips to slide smoothly down its coarse side. She could feel its skin under her touch. It felt like satin over sandpaper, slipping under the delicate touch of her fingertips. For a moment, the creature paused as if enjoying the brief contact and letting her know that everything was fine.

Edith turned with the camera toward Christin just as the last half of the creature's body passed between them. As soon as its tail cleared the gap, Edith could see the look of utter amazement and wonder in Christin's eyes and the smile on her lips, even with the regulator covering most of her lower face. They inched back together and grabbed each other's hands as they slowly turned and resumed their back-to-back posture, hovering in the rays of pale blue sunlight that penetrated the surface and illuminated the watery expanse filled with unwavering danger.

Christin greeted several more aquatic leviathans and a few minions as they mingled in a mass of deadly sea life. She even found enough bravery in her bones to look one particularly large hammerhead square in the eye, catching a glimpse of the totally empty depths of its gaze. She felt a cold chill deep in the pit of her stomach and a dreadful sorrow as if looking into the void of space and time itself. She regained her composure and looked down at the activity below her. Her gauges dangled at her side on a short tether, and it felt as if they had been visitors in this world for only a few minutes, but as she caught sight of her pressure gauge, she knew it was time to go or they would be in serious trouble. She reached back and poked Edith to get her attention. Edith turned slowly as Christin gave her a thumbs-up signal to return to the surface.

The two women began to rise and formed a single silhouette waltzing against the light of the sky above the waves. They held a long embrace at their decompression stops and finally ascended to the surface hand in hand.

The brave divers approached the ladder of the ship and climbed up to the deck above. Edith went first and reached down to help Christin pull her heavy gear onto the deck. Christin came over the side and planted her feet securely on the surface of the deck. She immediately turned and threw her head over the side and launched her breakfast into the briny deep. When she was done, she wiped her mouth off with her forearm and turned to sit on a deck box.

"Well, what do you think?" Edith inquired.

"THAT WAS FUCKING AWESOME!" Christin responded with childish glee. "I can't explain the feelings I had. I felt fear, horror, excitement, wonderment, solace, anxiety, joy, anger, and so much more, all at the same time! There is nothing like it in the world. That was amazing!"

"See, I knew you could do it. I knew you would like it once you got down there and got comfortable. You did great."

"When can we go back down?!"

"You know we have to decompress a little longer here topside and Rachel will probably want to move to a new location."

Christin turned toward the wheelhouse and with a huge smile, gave Rachel a big thumbs up which Rachel returned in like manner. She then collapsed on the deck in exhaustion as the weight of the experience washed over her while she came to grips with what she had done.

Never again in life could she experience those feelings. Like a drug, she wanted more. As the sun baked her fair skin, she could feel every muscle aching and she became dizzy. To die now would mean to die with a life fulfilled.

Chapter 20

A COLD RECEPTION IN WARM WATER

Rachel eased their aquatic home to a new anchorage location near the entrance to a cove next to a deadly-looking rock outcropping. This would be the next test of their mettle. It was time to dive closer to their final destination. Rachel decided to let Christin and Edith dive together one more time before taking her turn. She wanted to keep an eye out for the rangers and be prepared to deal with them should they take an interest in their activities.

Edith and Christin ate a light lunch and relaxed for a couple of hours to allow their bodies to decompress and recover. They prepped their gear and checked everything several times.

Rachel joined them on the deck as they relaxed, talking about life and people long gone. They rehashed the earlier experiences of the day and discussed how they would deal with a tragedy if something were to happen to one of them while on a dive. There was no medical care nearby, no decompression chamber for hundreds of miles, and no helicopter. Only the rangers could help if assistance was needed, and even they had limited resources to offer in this isolated Eden.

Christin was completely geared up before Edith was half done. She checked and rechecked her gear. Her hands once again shook uncontrollably but this time it was from excitement. Only a fleeting wisp of fear passed through her body as she prepared for her next dive.

Edith finally finished dressing as she positioned herself on the side of the ship in anticipation of slipping once again below the surface into the strange and deadly world of blues, grays, and greens. She glanced at Christin. "Well, are you ready to go?"

"You bet. Let's get wet." Christin leaned over and kissed Edith on the lips before pulling down her mask.

"You did brush your teeth, didn't you? You did just blow chunks a couple of hours ago."

"Yes, of course I did. After all, we don't want to add any chum to the water if we don't have to," Christin said as she winked at Edith through her mask.

As the two perched on the side rails, they looked out across the water and noticed that things appeared to be noticeably different here. They saw numerous fins cresting on the surf and quickly disappearing. The water seemed darker and less inviting. The island was casting a dark shadow over the area, giving the sea an even more ominous tone. Edith commented to herself on what a difference a few miles and a couple of hours can make.

Christin was the first one over this time. She plunged in and was overtaken by the euphoria of pure adrenaline. Edith entered far more reluctantly. Once again, the sharks scattered briefly upon their entrance but quickly regrouped in their aquatic ballet. Things seemed the same except for a few more sharks near the surface—many of them appeared to be much larger. The water was darker and less inviting. The currents took hold of the two and began playing a tug of war against every stroke of their fins. The two made eye contact and shared a brief "OK" sign as they began their descent into the depths.

They once again resumed their back-to-back posture as they began to mingle with the neighborhood's residents. It was immediately apparent that this neighborhood was not nearly as welcoming of outsiders. The sharks approached much faster and came much closer during their passes. The slightest touch or movement made them twitch and change direction. They circled in repeatedly and kept a watchful eye on these new intruders. Edith did not feel as safe this time. She directed Christin to move deeper so that they could get below this less tolerant school. Edith knew this could be a risky move since it could potentially cut off their most direct escape route.

As they descended below the frenzy, things began to calm down a bit. The women began slowly working their way along the reef wall toward a dark area in the near distance. As they got closer, several large sharks began to circle near them. They seemed agitated and unwelcoming. After a few minutes, they appeared to lose their patience with the daring duo and began moving in closer with each pass.

The girls inched closer toward the dark area and were suddenly whipped around in a whirlpool of current. One of the big sharks had glided in very close and gave them a powerful thrust from its tail fin. The movement of the water flipped the helpless duo around as if they were riding a tilt-a-whirl. They regained their bearings and noticed the large creature sitting motionless only a few feet away, its large black eyes staring at them, devoid of any emotion. The creature's icy gaze penetrated deep into their consciousness. Fear gripped both women as they joined the massive brute, hovering in a motionless standoff.

That approach was definitely a warning, Edith thought to

herself. She decided to push her luck a bit more to see what would happen. Would they receive another warning shot, or would they be met with a full-on attack? The possibility existed that they may even be allowed to continue forward. She had to know for sure. They inched another few feet in full view of the behemoth before them. Its vacant gaze tracked their every movement as it grew noticeably more agitated with every motion. The full length of its muscular 14-foot body twitched with anticipation. Suddenly, the beast could take no more and with a single powerful swish of its tail, bore down on them at full speed.

Christin did not have time to react to the event taking place. Her lack of intuition and inexperience caused her to freeze which impeded her ability to react. The full impact of the blow hit Christin square in the sternum and knocked the wind out of her. She winced in pain and she expelled her mouthpiece which began to free-flow and bubbled violently, every second wasting precious air. The final thrash of its tail pushed her against the jagged reef wall where she could feel the rocks and jagged outcroppings pushing into her back as her scuba tank scraped loudly against the hard surface. She was in trouble and she was panicking. She wanted to scream in pain and hyperventilate, but instinctively she knew that she couldn't. To do so would risk drowning.

Edith swam over and grabbed Christin by the arm. With her other hand, she grabbed Christin's regulator and placed it back into her mouth. She could see through the lens of Christin's goggles that she was in a lot of pain. Tears ran down her cheeks. Christin was hurt, scared, and in a lot of trouble.

Edith pulled Christin in close to embrace and comfort her when she suddenly felt an intense impact against her back. Luckily, her tank absorbed most of the blow, but it whipped her head back giving her a mild case of whiplash. The rush of water left in the creature's wake once again forced the pair against the jagged reef. This time Edith's arm took the major impact and she could feel the coarseness of the rocks against her skin. The rocks scraped and scratched their way through her wetsuit, leaving gashes down her arm. She could feel the saltwater stabbing her wounds. She could also see that the area around them was becoming tinged red with blood. The seawater filling her exposed wounds caused almost unbearable pain. Edith winced and squinted her eyes as she clenched down on her mouthpiece, nearly biting straight through it. Now they were both in serious trouble and the water was filling with the smell of blood.

Edith attempted to regain her composure. She was having difficulty managing her cognitive reasoning abilities. She could feel Christin trembling in her arms, so she concentrated on that as a point of focus.

After a few seconds, which felt like an eternity, Edith looked into Christin's fear-filled eyes. She immediately determined that they needed to surface. She had to save her friend, her lover, her soul mate, and her main reason for living. She pulled Christin in tight and turned to survey their surroundings. Through the faint pink glow of blood-tinged water, she could see three large sharks circling rapidly just a few feet away from their position. As each passed by, she could feel the force of these ill-tempered aggressors as they thrust their tails with fury, causing the water to surge past them. With each pass, it was if the ocean itself was closing in around them. Poseidon himself would quiver at the spectacle playing out in front of them.

Edith began to slowly kick her legs to keep from disturbing the waters unnecessarily. The last thing she wanted to do was to raise the ire of the mighty sentinels encircling them. They began to rise from the depths still in a full embrace.

Edith added a small amount of air to her buoyancy vest to help them ascend quicker. As they rose, the three protectors of this foreboding realm did not follow but maintained their vigilant watch over the eerie darkness of the reef wall. They kept a watchful eye on these two invaders as they slowly rose toward the surface.

Edith and Christin ascended cautiously to the first decompression stop. As they hung motionless in the open blue water they were constantly surrounded by as many as thirty circling hammerhead and tiger sharks. None of them approached or acted aggressively, even with the stench of human blood in the water. The sharks continued to circle, the whole time maintaining the same depth as the injured couple. After the final decompression stop, they continued to circle as if guiding them back to the safety of the ship and away from the realm that was truly theirs to rule. It was apparent that visitors who did not respect the law of the sea would pay a terrible price.

They had made it home.

Edith dragged Christin's nearly motionless body behind her. She climbed a couple rungs of the ladder and Rachel raced to the rail and reached over to grab the gear as Edith handed it to her. Piece by piece, she relieved their bruised and battered bodies of the heavy equipment. Soon, all that remained were the exhausted and tortured bodies of two of the strongest women Rachel had ever known. Seeing them struggle to climb the few remaining rungs of the ladder to reach the deck was more than she could bear, and she sobbed uncontrollably.

Both women settled on the deck in a shivering and inconsolable mass. Rachel embraced them both and kissed them repeatedly on the head. "I never meant for any of this to happen. I am such an ass. WHAT HAVE I DONE?!" she screamed for the entire world to hear as she wept.

The three huddled together for nearly ten minutes crying

and moaning. Finally, Christin fell back and lay on the deck. It was clear that the impact from the shark had bruised her sternum. As Rachel unzipped her wetsuit, she could see a large reddish-pink line extending across her torso. Rachel reached over and began probing the area for hidden damage. Christin moaned repeatedly and at one point moaned in agony as Rachel's strong fingers investigated a particularly angry and bruised area near a rib. "I am so sorry, Christin, but I need to know your condition. I don't think anything is broken, but I can't tell if there is any internal bleeding. I will need to radio this in and get you a medivac to a hospital."

Christin reached up with a quivering arm and touched Rachel's shoulder. "No, don't do that," she whispered. "I think I'm all right. It was just a warning. I'm just sore and shaken up a bit. I'll be okay. Just check on Edith."

By now Edith had gotten up and made her way to a first aid kit. She was clutching her arm with a towel to absorb the blood flowing from her wounds. A dark red stain was spreading through the once pristine white towel. Edith struggled to open the latch on the kit. Rachel squatted down next to her and opened the kit to reveal its contents. She rummaged through until she found several packets of betadine, gauze, and surgical tape. "Let me see the damage." Edith removed the towel to expose the wounded area of her arm.

"It doesn't look like you will need any stitches, but those are some nasty gashes and scrapes. I'm going to have to treat and dress them. I'm also going to have to give you a shot of antibiotic and a tetanus shot."

"I know the drill. Just patch me up, Cap'n. I need to get back to work and take care of my baby."

Edith managed only a slight grunt as Rachel poured the betadine into the wound and wiped it clean. She wrapped it in gauze and secured it with the surgical tape.

"Okay, turn around. Now for the unpleasant part."

"Any excuse to play with my ass. You know all you have to do is ask," Edith quipped, trying to add levity to the situation.

Rachel gave no answer. She plunged one needle deep into her left butt cheek and the other deep into her right butt cheek.

Rachel wiped the tears from her eyes. "Okay, there you go. Let's get Christin inside and let her lay down."

Rachel and Edith slowly lifted Christin to her feet and walked her into the berthing area. They helped her lie down on her rack, placed a pillow under her head, and covered her trembling body with a blanket.

Edith kissed Christin's forehead as she stroked her damp and salty red hair. "Are you okay? I am so sorry." Tears fell from Edith's eyes. This was the first time anyone had ever seen Edith cry.

"So, what the heck happened down there?" Rachel asked.

"We were greeted by the welcome wagon and neighborhood watch along with a couple of local thugs. Seems like they don't mind us being in their city, but there are certain neighborhoods where we don't belong," Edith replied.

"What do you mean?"

"Things aren't as friendly in this area. We were watched the whole time and when we tried to get near a dark area along the reef, we were abruptly pointed in a different direction and escorted out of the area by three burly brutes in gray suits. They roughed us up a bit and made sure we had a better understanding of our place in their world."

"That's it," Rachel said. "I am not risking anyone's life for a fool's quest. We are heading home in the morning at daybreak. Treasure or no treasure, it's not worth risking our lives. Get some rest, the sun is almost set. I'll make dinner in a few minutes."

"Okay, we aren't going anywhere."

Rachel left Edith to care for Christin as she returned to the wheelhouse. She sat in her chair as the last remaining traces of the day passed from existence. She wept quietly as she contemplated what was truly important in life.

Finally, the tears subsided and turned to salty crystals on her cheeks. She stared out into the darkness. Her mind was racing with a million thoughts but no direction. Her discontent was interrupted as she felt a hand on her shoulder. She turned to greet Edith but found no one there. She turned back to the darkness once more and allowed her mind to wander. As she sat deep in thought, a cool breeze washed over her body through the open window. She closed her eyes to soak in the comfort of the air. A few seconds later her thoughts were once again disrupted by a voice whispering in her ear, "They are not worthy without you. Come to me and guide them. No more harm will befall any of you if you do. Remember the full moon."

Rachel did not open her eyes. By now she knew the voice and she knew not to look for the source. She contemplated the words given to her and the warnings given to her crew. To leave now would mean to give up on all that they had worked so hard for, but it also meant that even if they were defeated, they could still go home and survive. Neither was a decision to be taken lightly and both carried grave consequences. Rachel needed time to consider the options. It was a full moon. Her stomach began to growl with hunger. She rose from her chair and made her way below to start dinner for her battered crew. Tomorrow would bring new questions and new answers.

Chapter 21

A TIME OF GREAT DECISION

Edith was sitting at the helm, reading a book and listening to music through her headphones, while Christin and Rachel slept. They had both had a rough night and Edith was glad to take a little extra time on watch to enjoy the peace and quiet of the morning. Her arm still throbbed a bit if she moved it the wrong way, but she was none the worse for wear from her ordeal.

Suddenly, she was nearly thrown to the floor as the silence was broken by the crackling of the radio and a familiar voice booming through the wheelhouse.

"*Lady Destiny,* this is Major Maria Aroza. Do you copy?"

Edith fumbled for the mic, knocking it from its holder and sending it careening into the panel below the radio. She was finally able to catch the violently swinging mic and press the button.

"Go ahead, Major, this is *Destiny.*"

"*Destiny,* we would like your crew to join us at our station post on the island for breakfast."

"That would be great, Major. Shall we dress for the occasion?"

The major replied with a distinct smile in her voice. "No, dress is not required, but we do recommend comfortable attire and walking shoes so we can conduct a proper tour."

"We will prepare our zodiac immediately," Edith responded.

"No need, *Destiny*. I will be sending a patrol boat to pick you up. We will arrive in half an hour."

"Roger that, Major. We'll be waiting."

Edith hung the mic back in its carrier and proceeded to the berthing area to wake Rachel and Christin.

Rachel was already getting out of her rack when Edith entered the room. "The major has invited us for breakfast, and I didn't dare say no." She then informed her when they'd arrive.

"I suspect that this is more than a social event and they'll search our boat while we're gone. We don't have much time, so let's get everything in order. Also, we need to hide the treasure maps for obvious reasons."

"I already thought of that. We can put them in one of the watertight gear canisters and tie it to the anchor line. We can let out extra line and the weight will hold the canister under the water while we are gone. Hopefully, they won't think to look there."

"I'll get everything in the canister while you get Christin out of bed." Rachel threw on a shirt and some deodorant before heading up to the wheelhouse.

Edith sat on the edge of Christin's rack and began stroking her cheek. "Hey, sleepyhead. Time to get up. We have an appointment with the police."

"So I heard. Help me sit up. I'm still a bit sore. At least I can breathe now, and I can tell that there isn't anything broken. Hand me a shirt so I can cover up the bruise. We don't want them asking stupid questions."

Edith handed Christin a pastel green T-shirt. Edith loved this shirt because it made Christin's green eyes almost glow when the light hit them just right. Christin slipped it on along with a pair of cut-off shorts and some deck shoes.

"That was uncomfortable. Wow it sure hurts if I bend over very far. I hope they don't ask us to dance," Christin said. Edith managed a tight smile as they headed topside.

Rachel had just finished stuffing the items into the canister as they arrived on deck.

"Everything's ready. Let's put it on the anchor line and at the same time we will put out a dive marker so they won't be suspicious. I'm sure they are watching us and we don't want them to know what we're doing."

Edith clipped the canister's carabiner to the chain while trying to keep it concealed as much as possible. At the same time, she dropped the dive marker buoy in a single fluid motion. Next, she began to slowly let out anchor chain so that it wouldn't be noticeable to anyone who might be watching.

After a few minutes, she ventured back inside to clean up before the patrol boat arrived.

Soon they heard the roar of an engine. The patrol boat was already closing in on their position by the time they made it to the rear deck to greet the ranger.

Edith grabbed a short, thin mooring line as the patrol boat nestled up next to them. She tied it off on the ranger's boat so they could board without too much difficulty. Rachel and Christin boarded together. Rachel held Christin's hand tightly to help support her weight as she stepped across. She hoped that it wouldn't be apparent to the ranger that Christin had been injured.

Edith grabbed a backpack along with a few extra items and then hopped across. Once her feet were firmly planted on the small patrol boat, she detached the line and cast off from the *Lady Destiny*.

Rachel had an uneasy feeling. She had never left her ship unattended anywhere except when they were docked in Gloucester. She made sure everything was secure and the engines were disabled before they left, but she still couldn't help feeling that something wasn't right.

Edith coiled the short line and turned around. "Hey, Ramone! How's it hanging?"

The young ranger grunted in displeasure and returned to the wheel. He pushed the throttles forward and they were off in an instant. They skipped across the tops of the swells for about ten minutes before arriving at a small pier.

Edith tied the bowline to the pier and helped Rachel and Christin off before disembarking herself.

Rachel took one step and immediately stumbled to her knees. "Ouch! That hurt."

"We have been at sea way too long. You may have great sea legs, but your land legs could use some work." Edith chuckled.

"I'm not used to my feet being planted on something that doesn't move under me all the time. It's like learning to walk all over again."

"Come on, pick your ass up and let's go. Ramone's leaving us in the dust," Edith said as she offered a helping hand.

The small band of explorers, along with their guide, arrived at the ranger station around 9:30. Set before them was a modest wooden table situated in a small garden area surrounded by palm trees. Upon it was a spread of colorful and delectable foods fit for a king. Major Aroza appeared through the door of the station carrying a large tray. "Good morning, Captain. I would like to welcome you and your crew to our humble outpost."

Rachel smiled at the sight and quickly responded, "Thank you, Major. We really appreciate your invitation, and I would not call this humble. This is one of the most beautiful places I have ever seen. May we assist you with anything?"

"No, this is the last of it. We are glad to have you join us. We don't get to cook such elaborate meals for guests very often. We just received a supply delivery and we wanted to share it with you since you have traveled so far to be with us. After being at sea for so long, we knew you would appreciate a good meal."

Christin said, "This looks amazing and it smells spectacular. I love to cook. I have to have those recipes!"

"These are simple dishes prepared by the other rangers and me. We each have a specialty that we like to prepare."

"I have also brought a little something along for you," Christin said. "Yesterday, while we were decompressing from a dive, I made a pineapple-mango upside-down cake with a lemon glaze. And I brought a bottle of rum I picked up in Panama." Christin began rifling through the backpack Edith had been carrying. First, she pulled the bottle of dark rum with a label she couldn't read and then the golden-brown dense cake that she had prepared in a loaf pan. The glaze shimmered in the sunlight as she pulled off the plastic wrap protecting it.

"Now, that is a treat! We don't get many cakes or baked goods out here since they don't provide much sustenance and they don't keep well in the humidity."

"You're going to love this, then. It is nothing but bad for you. I also soaked it in a bit of rum for extra flavor. It was no easy trick hiding it from these two and it's a little lopsided."

"Thank you, Christin. We appreciate this gesture. Now, please, take a seat and join us."

The trio and two young officers took seats on the opposite side from the major and her senior officers.

They enjoyed a meal of fresh fish over rice with mango salsa, fresh fruit, and a delicate quiche-like dish that wasn't quite a quiche and wasn't quite anything else, but it tasted fantastic.

They ate until they couldn't hold another bite. They each drank coffee and finished the meal with a shot of Christin's special rum and a piece of her decadent pineapple cake.

The meal was cordial and friendly which was a huge departure from their last meeting on board the *Lady Destiny*.

"We hope you are enjoying your visit to our sanctuary. Have you had any trouble since you arrived?" the major inquired.

"Nothing really. We did a morning dive to get Christin used to diving with sharks which was truly remarkable. Later in the afternoon we moved to our current location and did a second dive. We noticed that the sharks are a little more aggressive over there, so we kept that one short," Edith commented.

"Yes, we have known about the behavior of those sharks in that area. We aren't sure what causes it, but it is best to play it safe. We recommend diving away from that location even though it has some of the best underwater formations and more unique sea life. It is also where the biggest sharks tend to congregate if you like the adrenaline rush from diving with them."

"We mainly hung to the reef, so we didn't have an open side for them to sneak up on us. A swell came in and pushed us around a bit and I got scraped up on the reef."

"Would you like our medic to look at it? We don't want you getting sick out here or getting an infection."

"Rachel fixed me up, gave me an antibiotic and tetanus shot, but I would be happy to have your medic take a look."

The major nodded to one of her staff. He rose and walked over to where Edith was sitting. He removed her dressings and looked at her wounds intently. After a moment he walked into the station and re-emerged with a few items. He applied an ointment to her wounds and rewrapped her arm with a fresh dressing gauze.

Edith looked up as he finished and gave the medic a pleasant smile. He smiled back and nodded in appreciation of her gesture. He gathered his few things and returned to the station building.

"So, is there anything in particular you were expecting from your visit with us and our sanctuary?"

Rachel flashed a quick smile. "No, we just wanted to get away to a tropical island that wasn't overrun with tourists. We were looking at a few maps and this one stood out to us, even though we could barely see it on the chart. We did a little research and once the fishing season was over, we set our course. We thought a diving vacation would be everything we needed to re-energize and relax. We were hoping to see a bit more of the island. We haven't been on firm ground very much this year, so we take advantage of any opportunity to come ashore."

"Major, I hope you don't mind, but may I ask how you and your officers came to be rangers here? Seems to me that this duty could be wonderful but also very lonely," Edith inquired.

"Most of us are here by choice. Much of the work on the mainland is very physical and it doesn't pay much. Most Costa Ricans relish any opportunity they may be offered to get away from the grueling dangerous field work or the meager living provided by jobs in the tourism or service industries. To be a government ranger is something that we do not take lightly and most of us have sacrificed comfort and family for a chance at a somewhat more secure albeit lonely occupation."

"We can appreciate that choice. I have a lot of respect for anyone who would put themselves in danger to be stewards of Cocos. But what about you? Due to your education and upbringing, you seem to have more opportunities than most. Why are you here?" Rachel asked as she shoved another bite of Christin's cake into her mouth.

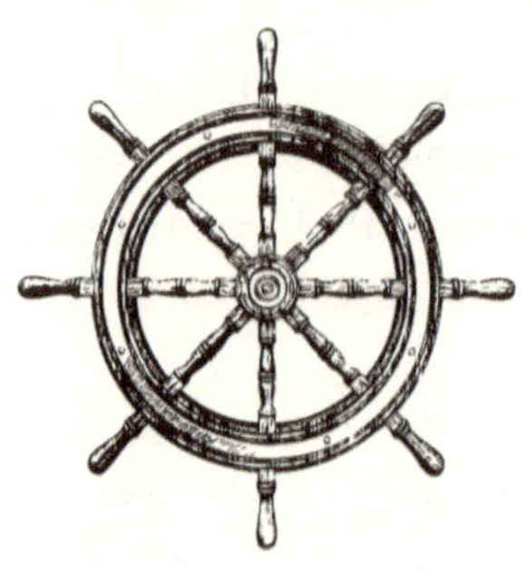

Chapter 22

SHOES TO FILL

"When I was a little girl, my father was an ecologist for the government. He would be gone for long periods conducting his work. When I became a little older, he would take me along on some of his local trips. I loved to visit the mountains and forests to view and study the animals with him, but I really loved the beach. On one trip we went snorkeling together over a coastal reef. I was about fourteen at the time without a care in the world. While we snorkeled, I felt intense pain in my ears and a sickness in my stomach. My head throbbed and I felt like I wasn't going to make it back alive. I squinted as I tried to breathe heavily. When I opened my eyes there was a large tiger shark in front of me staring into my eyes. I trembled with fear and I couldn't move. He also did not move and hung motionless. I could see my father approaching from the distance. I reached out my hand and touched the nose of that great beast and when I did my pain stopped and was replaced by beautiful music."

Edith stopped chewing on a piece of fresh papaya as she became engrossed in Maria's story.

"I know this sounds stupid and like I am making it up, but I assure you that it is true."

Christin spoke. "Please don't stop. I love your story. I want to hear more. What happened to the shark and your dad?"

"The shark twitched when I made contact just as my father was getting close. It turned its head and gave a mighty swish of its tail which sent my father tumbling through the water and into its depths. The mighty beast swam away to a distance and lurked at the edge of my vision. As my father tumbled through the water he gasped for a breath and inhaled two lungs full of water. He went limp and I dove to catch his hand. I grasped onto his hand for dear life. My fins struggled against his weight as I fought to bring him to the surface. Once I got him above water, I spent the next several minutes getting him to shore. By this time a few people on the beach witnessed our predicament and went to get help. I worked on him for about half an hour before the medics arrived. He had a weak pulse and was barely breathing when they took him to the hospital."

Maria wiped a tear from her eye before continuing. "He died three days later. I loved my father and from that time on, I knew I wanted to follow him and become an ecologist and protector of all creatures. A few weeks after his funeral, my mother and I returned to the beach where my father had his encounter with the shark. I took a wreath of flowers and snorkeled out to the place where it happened. The moment I entered the water I heard the beautiful music once more. I felt content and I released the flowers so the waves could carry them away. I floated on the surface for several minutes watching the wreath drift into the distance. As I began to lose sight of it, it was replaced by a dark shadow approaching from below me. In a few seconds I was once again face to face with the very same behemoth that caused my father's demise. I did not feel fear or anger as I stared into the vacant black voids of its expressionless eyes. This time when I reached out my hand to touch it, it bowed its head slightly and slid slowly beneath me as I caressed the length of its body. A few seconds later it was alongside me. Its gnarly toothed grin was only inches from me. It nudged me slightly with its nose as if telling me it was time to move on before it swam effortlessly toward the deep blue of the open ocean."

Maria handed her plate to one of the junior officers as he cleared the table. She smiled at him and returned to her story without skipping a beat. "I found out my father frequently traveled to this island for his work. I studied the history of the island and the folklore that surrounds it. I became obsessed with its unique ecology and bio-diversity, and I knew it would be a good place to connect with my father, so I went to school in LA on an exchange program with the help of a scholarship and a lot of hard work. When I graduated, I immediately applied with the Costa Rican Park Services to become a ranger. Many of the senior officials still remembered my father and were eager to make me an offer. That was eleven years ago. During that time I served in many locations until I got the opportunity to come to this island. They couldn't imagine a woman wanting to serve as a ranger in this place, but I jumped at the opportunity and the promotion. For two years now I have commanded this small team while also serving as the island's chief biologist. I call this island home. My mother died just before I was transferred here and now this is all I have. I have explored much of the accessible parts of the island and I have delved deep into its history. I feel a connection to this place like I have a calling to be here. When I swim in the sea, I still here the songs playing in my ears, as if the Sirens that protect this place are singing directly to me and guiding me to my destiny. I am content and happy here even though it can be lonely, but when I have feelings of self-doubt or loneliness, I go to a special place that sits above the water where I can peer into the depths and lose myself to the sea breeze. If you like, I will take you there and show you around the island."

"That would be fantastic. We would love to see it. We are sorry for your loss and loneliness, but it seems you have found a way to cope and connect with your father. I pray that you have happy days down the road," Edith responded in a hushed tone.

"I don't know what my future holds, but I do know that my place is here with my family and the legacy they have left me. Sometimes I see great joy in my future and at other times I see great sadness playing on its heels. I am glad that this is one of those moments of great joy. Thank you for visiting our island and being a part of its story. Maybe one day you will find that you have a connection to this place much like I have."

"I think we already feel a connection to the island and its history, and I hope we have made a friend in you, Major. You and I have had nearly identical experiences in our lives. I, too, lost my father to the sea when I was young. I have followed in his footsteps and I strive every day to carry on his legacy. In a way, I think that his legacy is what led us here. I feel that he has guided me through life and will push me in ways I would not normally go. I think he knew the girls and I needed to come to this place to relax and make a connection with the world and find a kindred spirit in you." Rachel clasped Maria's hand in solidarity. They were both their fathers' daughters who had grown into very independent and capable women. From that moment Rachel knew that she and Maria were meant to cross paths, and in some small way share in this quest.

"It is almost like we were meant to find each other in this isolated place. I have never revealed my past to anyone that I barely know before, but I feel comfortable around the three of you and it is a wonderful relief to finally share my story with people who can understand what I have been through. Well, enough with the mushy stuff. I don't go on duty for a few more hours so I would be glad to show you around."

"That would be great. Let us help you clean up first," Christin replied.

"Thank you, but my officers will help with that. Follow me and I will show you around."

The trio stood, shook hands, and thanked the other rangers for a wonderful breakfast and pleasant company, leaving them to devour the rest of the alcohol-laden cake without the major watching over them.

Chapter 23

ALONG THE PATHS OF THOSE
WHO CAME BEFORE

The major and her small posse of women departed from the table and proceeded to cross the courtyard toward a narrow path that led into the thick rainforest. As they approached the beginning of the trail, the major picked up several large sticks and handed one to each of them. "These will help you during the hike, especially if your land legs are not steady. They will also serve as protection if we should run into any wild pigs. We have many on the island and they can be very aggressive."

"Really? What are wild pigs doing here?" Christin asked.

"Many years ago, when sailors and pirates frequented the island, they brought three things with them: pigs and goats for food, and rats that escaped their ships. All three took over the island and are scourges on our ecosystem. Stay close and we should be fine. I also have my gun if we need it. This trail can be a bit treacherous, so if you aren't up to it, let me know and we will take a shorter trail that is equally as beautiful."

"We are all fit, but we haven't been off the boat in a while, so the shorter hike might be a little better for me," Christin said.

"Okay, Christin, we will take the shorter trail then. Let's go."

As the small group made their way through the rain forest, the major pointed out many of the local birds and animals native to the island, explaining its geology and unique ecological identity. She regaled them with stories of pirate lore and the antics of early visitors to the island. She also told them how it was believed that the island was thought to have been the inspiration for Robert Louis Stevenson's *Treasure Island*.

They meandered down the winding trail going ever higher until suddenly the major stopped and motioned everyone to be quiet. In the distance, they could see a wild pig rooting near a tree. They watched it with guarded attention for what seemed to be an eternity. It finally moved on, leaving their path clear. They were free to continue their expedition into the secrets of Cocos Island.

They had hiked nearly a mile and a half when they abruptly emerged from the forest onto a rocky outcropping far above the ocean below. The view was spectacular and left the trio nearly speechless. Christin was deathly afraid of heights and was having a hard time venturing near the edge for a better view. The scene before them and the cool sea breeze helped to put her fears at ease, and she was able to inch her way out to where the others were standing. Down below, they could see the surf kissing the coastline. The emerald green of the island's mountainous terrain stood in stark contrast to the blue hues of the surrounding waters.

"This is my quiet spot. I come here to gather my thoughts and refresh my soul. It is also a great place to observe the many dive boats that venture here. Like those two over there and yours anchored just below us. Those other two just arrived from the mainland a few hours ago."

"This is truly an amazing place, Major," Rachel stated in awe.

"This is my home and I will protect it to my dying breath. My job is not easy. I must fight off poachers and treasure hunters, as well as deal with the issues brought about by the many tourist and dive boats that arrive here every week. But here I can find peace and the world looks peaceful. I sometimes come up here and imagine that I was once a pirate who stood in this very spot before burying my treasure in the bowels of the island. Here, the ancient spirits of the island speak to me in the wind and the sound of the waves, and I find meaning in my life. I think that is part of the reason my father came here so often. I think it was a way for him to connect to Yemayá, the Mother of the Sea, and to the world around him. I think my family has long had an obligation to this place and to protect the secrets it holds."

"We envy you. It is a gift to be able to enjoy this beautiful place whenever you want, but we don't envy your job."

"Thank you, Edith. This is a blessing and a curse all at once. The beauty is wonderful, but the isolation is torment. I am bound by an obligation to perform a duty, which I do happily, but I also miss the few friends I have on the mainland, and the comforts of civilization. I cannot have a relationship here unless it is with one of my officers, which is forbidden. I think of it as the joy of loneliness. I have a duty and obligation to this island and its history. Most would not and do not understand what that means to me. I fear that one day it will be my fate to die here, but then, there isn't a more beautiful place to find your final peace."

"I don't think I could ever do your job," Christin whispered.

"It takes a special person to want to do this every day.

Many rangers do not know what to expect when they take this assignment and they burn out quickly." Suddenly the major pointed out into the blue sea. "Look out there! Do you see that large dark mass over there with the white specs?"

"Yes!" the three said in unison.

"That is a school of rays and the white specs occur when they throw their massive bodies out of the water and come splashing back down. They throw themselves into the air to clean their bodies and remove parasites like remora. You need to try and dive with them this afternoon. They should stay in the area for a while, so you should have time."

"That sounds amazing. What is that dark mass over there?"

"That looks like a school of hammerhead or tiger sharks. They can be extremely aggressive. We have had a fair number of people injured and killed here from shark attacks, so be careful. This is a dangerous place, but it is one of the most beautiful places you will ever dive. Let's head back down, so you can get a dive in with the rays this afternoon."

"Sounds good to me. I'm ready and I got a lot of great pictures," Edith said excitedly.

The group headed back down a different trail past large waterfalls and beautiful meandering streams. Before long they were back at the ranger station. They were greeted by the intense heat of the afternoon sun as they emerged from the protection of the jungle canopy.

"One of my officers will take you back to your vessel now. I am sure we will see each other again soon. Be safe and don't be foolish. Too many visitors leave here in cuffs or bandages and sometimes the occasional body bag. Don't be one of those. Respect the island and it will be good to you. Mistreat it or break the rules and you will pay a heavy price."

Rachel reached out her hand to the major. "Thank you for your hospitality. We appreciate your time and the lessons you have given us about the island and its history. I hope one day we can join you again for another adventure here."

The major reached her outstretched hand toward Edith. Edith grabbed it firmly and yanked the unsuspecting ranger close to give her a huge hug, wrapping the ranger in her muscular arms. "It's been great, Major. Thank you so much."

Christin cast a sideways glance at Edith for a split second. Once her brief hint of jealousy had subsided, she also gave the major a light and polite hug, being careful not to expose her bruises. "Thank you very much, Major. Don't forget to get me a copy of those recipes."

"I won't. Be safe, ladies. It has been a pleasure to spend time with such kindred spirits. As the old pirates used to say, 'Beware the song of the Sirens. They will lead you to your doom.'"

They exchanged final waves on the pier as they cast off and returned to their ship.

When they boarded the *Lady Destiny*, they found everything was just as they had left it. Once the patrol boat cleared the corner and was out of sight, Edith pulled up the anchor chain a bit and reclaimed the tube with its precious contents.

It was now late in the afternoon and they needed to work fast to get a dive in.

"So, I guess we're staying?" Edith directed at Rachel.

"Yes, we're staying. Someone here doesn't want us to leave yet. Prep my gear, too. I'm going down with you guys this time."

"Who's going to take care of the ship if we are all down below?" Christin asked while sporting a puzzled look.

"No worries. The ship is in good hands and the Sirens are also watching. By the way, we aren't chasing any rays on this dive."

Chapter 24

THE TIDES OF CHANGE ARE WITH US

The three were decked out and geared up in no time. They double-checked each other's gear and with an "OK" sign from Rachel, they leaned back and slipped into the warm blue waters.

Rachel rolled over away from the surface and for an instant, she froze. She had never seen so many sharks in one place. They were everywhere. Big ones, little ones, tigers, hammerheads. Some were so big they looked as if they could swallow a person whole. A few rays slid past the women, separating them from the menacing masses below.

Edith got everyone's attention and they exchanged the customary "OK" sign. Edith led them downward into the darkening depths. As they descended, a massive hammerhead began advancing slowly upwards to meet them. He was accompanied by an entourage of twenty or more sharks of various types.

In a matter of seconds, the gap closed to only a couple of feet. The entourage circled below in an excited manner as if they were trying to create an impenetrable layer of living steel. Christin immediately recognized the biggest one that was staring them down. It was the same shark that had rammed her yesterday. The two groups were once again in a standoff. Neither would yield to the other and the tension created by the stalemate was palpable.

Edith glanced over toward Rachel who was frozen in place. She was staring deep into the big shark's soul-draining eye. After a moment, she began slowly swimming forward until she was only inches away and eye to eye with the motionless leviathan before her. She presented the exquisite bracelet she received from her grandfather's chest to the massive guardian of the deep as proof that she was entitled to pass and gain entrance into the mysteries that lay beyond the beast's hulking mass. She reached out her hand further and touched its head ever so gently. As she made contact, the shark appeared to lower its head as if bowing before her.

At the very instant of first contact, the ocean became awash in the sounds of a powerful choral aria. All three women reacted with startled surprise. The lead shark slowly turned and headed back down and straight toward the dark area they had been so intent on defending the day before. As he passed through the circling mass of sharks, the entourage seemed to form an orderly line on both sides of his path. He had essentially opened a clear passage for these visitors from the world above.

Once the lead shark had reached the dark area, he turned toward the trio and hung suspended in the blackness around him, as if inviting them to advance. He moved ever so slightly as the currents caused him to sway back and forth. His movements were just enough to keep water flowing over his gills to oxygenate his blood.

Rachel went first. She led the other two past the

gauntlet of tiger sharks, hammerheads, and various other species until she was once again eye to eye with the massive protector of the darkness. Now the choir was even louder. Rachel again reached out and touched the head of the big shark. This time he arched his back and began to ascend above them as if removing the final obstacle that lay between them and what was previously forbidden.

Once the entire length of the shark's body had passed, Rachel again began to descend into the blackness. As she got closer, she realized that a large rock, really a monolith, created the blackness—it harbored no life upon it and re-flected no light. It was as big as two school buses parked side by side. It was another obstacle that appeared to be insur-mountable. Rachel swam across its surface and touched it with her hand. The blackness was so deep that she could not judge her distance from it. The monolith harkened mem-ories back to the old Stanley Kubrick film, *2001: A Space Odyssey.*

She began to swim along its perimeter to study its every detail. At one outcropping near the top, she could see a six-foot moray eel hiding among the other stones and con-cretions. Starfish, anemones, and urchins dotted the reef wall around the black monolith but not the monolith it-self. Various small fish darted in and out of crevices around the blackness but refused to pass in front of it. Corals and anemones decorated the reef with a living display of grace-ful beauty; in the waning light, she could see the area around the monolith was exploding with color and life. The delicate corals and sea fans swayed fluidly in the slowly rolling surf, like a baby's cradle under a mother's caring hand.

Rachel continued along the perimeter with Edith and Christin trailing behind. She was now advancing down the left side of the irregular-shaped monolith toward its bottom edge. She could see little detail at the full depth of this ebony structure. She retrieved her flashlight and shined it around the area. At the very bottom left corner, she spotted an opening about three feet by four feet that appeared to stretch back behind the mammoth stone. She shined her light inside but could not completely comprehend what she was seeing. It appeared that the walls of the opening were moving. At that moment a small fish, similar in shape to a large mullet, darted into the opening. Then a rush of water expelled from the opening. Rachel could see massive jaws entrap and devour the small prey. She now realized that she was looking into the den of a grouper weighing several hundred pounds with its mouth agape. It appeared to be the size of a cow but moved with the grace of a ballerina.

Once her heart stopped pounding, Rachel reached for the strike stick dangling from her gear and proceeded to try and coax the monstrous fish from its home. The prodding of the stick angered the giant fish and it let out a deafening throng that hurt the ears of the three women. It even drowned out the choral theme playing in their ears. Once the thronging stopped, Rachel again began to prod at the fish until it reluctantly left its burrow.

Once the massive grouper's cavity was evacuated, she could see deeper inside the opening. The walls were covered with crabs and warm water lobsters as well as a myriad of other unidentifiable creatures. Rachel could also see that the darkness extended far beyond the reach of her flashlight. She turned to Edith and Christin, gave them the "OK" sign, and then pointed inside the opening.

Rachel slid cautiously into the opening, being careful not to catch any of her hoses or gear on the jagged walls. Before long, the entire length of her body was inside.

Christin followed her at a safe distance and Edith brought up the rear.

Rachel's flashlight continued to pierce the darkness but to no avail, as the darkness appeared to absorb all the light that was emitted. The music of the sea continued to become louder and louder as they swam down the tight passage, deeper and deeper into the belly of the island.

It seemed as if they had traveled for an eternity, but she knew it must have been no more than a hundred feet or so before they arrived inside a large open chamber. Rachel spun slowly, casting her light in all directions. She was moderately disoriented and pointed her light in a direction that she thought was up. She could see what appeared to be ripples. She advanced rapidly toward the geometric patterns above her until; finally, her head emerged from the water into an open cave. She again cast her light around the space to find some feature that she could use as a reliable reference for her position. To the front and right of her appeared to be a small sandy beach area perched on a large rock. She got her bearings and swam toward it.

Edith and Christin emerged from the desolate depths just behind Rachel and followed her to the sandy area. Rachel pulled herself up onto the sand and removed her mouthpiece and mask to test the air. Once she was satisfied that it was acceptable to breathe the air, she helped her friends up onto the small beach area. The whole sandy patch was barely big enough to accommodate their combined size and gear.

Rachel leveled her light at the other two women to check their condition. "Are you two okay?"

"Yeah, I'm fine, but I think Christin is pretty scared. I can feel her shaking."

"I am scared and a bit cold," said Christin. "I don't like

this place. It gives me the creeps. Not to mention that my BC is putting a lot of pressure on my bruises and it hurts like hell. Now, what do we do? I don't hear the music anymore. What was that anyway?!"

"I think it was the song of the Sirens," Rachel replied.

"Oh, come on. You don't believe that bullshit, do you?"

"Edith, at this point I would believe anything. I do know one thing. This isn't the end of our quest. There has to be something more to it than an empty chamber."

The three women moved their lights around the space trying to find a clue to their next steps. Rachel's light caught the shape of a large rock that cast a shadow alongside it. "Do you see that? It looks like that rock may be set a small distance from another opening. I'm going to wiggle back and see what's there."

Rachel slid her slender frame next to the rock and found a narrow opening behind it. She couldn't see how far back it went, but she could fit her body into the opening without too much trouble. Once she had gotten nearly halfway in, she let out a loud, blood-curdling scream. "Aaauugh!!!" She scrambled back to the others. Her hands trembled as they fought to hold the light.

"What's wrong?!" Christin screamed in an unsteady tone, her voice cracking in the darkness.

"It's a human skull. We are on the right path. That just scared the shit out of me." Rachel took a moment to catch her breath. "Okay, I think we can get through there, but we will have to drag our gear. It's too small to walk or crawl. Let's go."

"Wait a minute! Go where? We don't know where we are going," Christin said stiffly.

"I do know where I'm going." Her voice was heavy with conviction. "I studied that map for hours and I know every twist and turn. The beach was a symbol on the map. The corner around the rock is shown on the map. Even the skull was shown on the map in a simple symbol of dots and a few vertical lines. Now I realize it was the representation of a skull with teeth. Not to mention, I can still hear the songs of the Sirens. I have no choice but to go on. If you want to stay here then stay, but I must go on or I'll be haunted forever by the thought of what might have been and the realization that I failed at fulfilling my ancestral obligation. I don't blame you if you don't want to go on. I'm scared, too."

"Okay, if you are that sure, we aren't going to let you go alone. I'll follow you."

"If Christin is following you, then I'm coming, too. Let's go."

The three proceeded to wiggle themselves and their equipment through the narrow hole. After about twenty feet or so, the opening made a sharp turn to the right. After another six feet, the opening led into a large chamber about the size of an average house.

Rachel pulled herself through and into the open chamber. She helped the others through, and they set their gear next to the side of the opening to mark its location in the darkness.

They once again searched the room for anything that might have meaning. Along the wall to their left was a knee-deep freshwater pool which was fed by a small waterfall extending from a crack in the ceiling of the chamber. In the center was an elevated area that appeared to have been worn smooth over time, but by what? In the far wall were two more openings that were large enough to walk through.

The three made their way over to the openings and contemplated which to take. Rachel's light scanned the floor and they noticed strange markings on the smooth surface of the stone under their feet. Edith moved back and shined her lantern across the surface so the markings would cast a shadow. Christin and Rachel did the same. Soon the entire surface was illuminated in relief and a message could be read.

Those who venture here must choose their path. Life or Death.

Christin looked at Edith. "Which one?"

"How should I know?"

"I know," Rachel replied in a hushed voice.

"You know? How do you know? Was it spelled out on your precious little map, too?" Christin snipped.

"No, hear me out. Ancient sailors looking for treasure were lured to their death by the songs of the Sirens. Those sailors were all men who could not resist the seductions of the water nymphs."

"Well, we aren't men!"

"Exactly, Edith. We aren't men, so we can't be lured to our deaths. I can still hear the Sirens' songs and they are coming from the cave to the right, so we will go left."

"That makes sense. Your quirky intuition has gotten us this far. Let's go with it. What the hell. There are a thousand ways to die down here, and I am willing to follow you if it means we have a better chance to survive this," Christin blurted confidently.

"Okay, left it is. Lead on, Rachel. Christin trusts you, so I trust you."

They picked up their lanterns and proceeded cautiously into the left cave. The deeper they went, the quieter the songs became until they were replaced by the sounds of rushing water. Finally, Rachel found relief from the constant torment of the Sirens' songs. After about a hundred feet, they entered another open chamber that was slightly smaller than the last. On the far wall was another wild waterfall forming a small stream that swept past their feet. In the center of the room was another elevated area of smooth rock. There were no other visible features. The space was empty and void of anything except the waterfall, the stream, the elevated area, and the path they followed in.

"So, this is it?" snapped Edith in disgust. "We came all this way to find an empty room. We took the wrong path. I'm going back."

"No, don't. I know this is right. We are just missing something." Rachel grasped the pendant hanging around her neck. She clenched it between two fingers and shined her light on it. "What are we missing?! What did we do wrong?!" she exclaimed. She glanced at the stone in the center and noticed something odd. Through the opening in the stone of her geode pendant, she could see the light from the other flashlights in the room, but the images did not match.

"I don't think that old thing is going to help us much anymore," exclaimed Edith.

Rachel pulled the stone to her eye and peered through it like a monocle. The room became awash with misty apparitions. At that instant, a deep hollow moan tore through the space and shook the women to their core.

"What the hell was that?" Christin cried fearfully.

Rachel continued to study the new landscape before her. Suddenly their dive lanterns all flickered and faded to black. There they stood, together in the darkness with no light, no references, and no way out.

Nearly two long minutes had gone by when a faint glow filled the room from above. They had overlooked a small opening in the ceiling of the chamber and light was streaming in through it, but what was the source?

Christin was the first to ask, "So where is that light coming from?"

"I don't know," said Edith.

"The full moon," Rachel whispered. "It's the light of the full moon entering through a shaft to the surface."

Another haunting moan was heard which then became intelligible. "Welcome, granddaughter," it said in a raspy, haunting voice.

"Granddad Kristiansen, is that you?"

A ghostly haze began to form in the moonlight above the smooth rock. Slowly, the figure of a man dressed in garb similar to those of the ancient deckhands of pirate lore appeared to the fearful trio. The apparition swayed back and forth as if submerged in shallow surf, occasionally disintegrating into a fine mist and then remerging into distinct features.

"Yes, granddaughter, I am here. I have always been here."

"How did you know it was me?"

"Simple, my child," the voice whispered. "You are the only one who may enter here. You followed my map and read the clues to find this place. This is my prison tomb and it is my destiny to protect the cursed treasure hidden within. Anyone else who would dare to enter this chamber would instantly die and be swept away by the waters that protect this realm and isolates our two worlds."

"Cursed treasure? What do you mean cursed treasure? There isn't anything here!" snapped Edith.

"You seek treasure of a physical nature, yet you cannot see what lies all around you. This treasure is not of your world. It is of mine, Edith."

"How do you know me?" Edith asked trembling.

"I have known you and Christin as long as you have been in this world. I have watched you grow up and I have known the bond you three share. I have seen it through

Rachel's eyes and before that, through Gwen's. I sent messages and recruited Rachel's father when all was in peril."

"You killed my father!" exclaimed Rachel.

"No, he didn't," said a familiar man's voice from behind Rachel's shoulder. "Our family has a unique legacy, Rachel. We are sworn at birth to protect our family and serve the sea at all costs. I went to meet your grandfather willingly as a part of my duty and oath to the sea."

A second figure began to coalesce as a fine mist rushed past Rachel and passed over the small stream flowing in the space. It finally stopped on the smooth rock and turned to face Rachel. This figured moved and swayed in unison with the first, but its mists were a sharp blue hue with fine wisps of silver and gray.

"Daddy?" Rachel choked out through her tears.

"Yes, my girl. I have watched you grow up all these years. You have heard my voice in the wind, felt my touch in the sun, and known my love always in your heart. Your grandfather and I have guided you and pushed you to be who you are. Now, you must answer the same call we have both succumbed to. You are a child of the sea and I love you dearly. Once more our family is in peril and it requires a protector from the living realm."

"So, why did you leave me?"

The figure moved around the center of the room, finally stopping slightly in front of and next to the other ghostly figure. "I didn't. I was taken from you while protecting our legacy. There is one who took his ill-gotten gains and buried them here. He then betrayed his crew and left them here to die. Your grandfather escaped and vowed to settle the score. He entered a pact with Odin and the sea. For ages, he tracked down the scoundrel who would exile his own men to an early grave. In return, Odin placed his own curse on the treasure. Until the score is settled and an heir to the rightful crew can answer the call, all will be in service to the sea and bound to protect the treasure in this vile place of dark despair."

Through her tears, Rachel could clearly see her father's outline and she still knew his voice. "I have missed you so much, Daddy. I knew you were there. I tried to learn your lessons. Now that I am here, the curse is broken. You can come home."

"It isn't that easy, my child. Our vow has not yet been fulfilled. You must serve the same oath as every captain in our family's legacy."

"I don't understand."

"The scallywag that doomed his crew still haunts this earth and until he is gone the curse cannot be broken."

"But Grandfather was not the captain of the *Relampago*. He was the quartermaster."

"Yes, Granddaughter. I was the quartermaster but to most of the crew, I was the rightful captain and the one they trusted with their lives. In the end, I did not fulfill my duties to them and now I serve Odin in recompense for my failings."

"What do I have to do?" Rachel sniffled.

"Assume the vow and serve the sea at our side. Only an ancient family trinity can defeat the monster who holds us in this curse. Three common captains forming a single bond to conquer an ancient curse."

"I will do it if it will set you free."

"To remove our bindings to this curse, you must cross the stream and join us here, as the third of our family trinity."

"I will."

"Hey, wait just a minute, Rachel! You might not ever

be able to come back, and we can't lose you!" Christin cried out.

"Whether in life or in death, I will always be here for you. My love for you is as great as that for my family. Right now, I must choose what is right and I choose to end this curse and serve my family and the sea. I must end the torment that plagues my family and weighs on my shoulders and those of my ancestors. Wait here for me…please. Just wait for me here."

Edith grabbed Rachel firmly and held her tight. With all her might she tried to keep Rachel from moving from her place, but Rachel was determined. She took a step into the stream and then another. Edith struggled to hold on. She fought to keep her friend, her family, and her sister from leaving her. Rachel took another step and her hand evaporated from Edith's grasp as she was absorbed into the moonlight. Edith stood there with her empty hand extended, frozen in the moment. Christin turned away and hid her face as she sobbed.

Chapter 25

FOR FAMILY

Rachel joined her family and stood at her father's side. In the trinity, they would find their final destiny and the curse that was cast upon her family would once and for all be broken. Her ghostly apparition shown with an intensity of yellow light that nearly blinded Edith and Christin. Rachel embraced her father and cried on his shoulder. She kissed the face she had not known since that fateful day so long ago. Next, she turned to embrace her great-great-grandfather whom she had never known, but, somehow, had always known. She could smell his breath. It was as sweet as the vanilla that accompanied her dreams and the happiest of times in Gwen's home. His home, first.

As Rachel embraced her grandfather, an eerie sound flooded the chamber. There was no way to know where it was coming from since it seemed to come from everywhere at once. It sounded as if someone were beating a large metal hammer against hard stone. Scraping, banging, and unnerving sounds that could reach into a person's soul and immobilize them with fear.

Rachel's grandfather handed her a sword. "You will need this, my love. It is all up to you now. Help us to end this curse and put us to rest so that we may finally find peace and this beast might be damned to the bowels of hell for eternity."

Rachel grasped the sword firmly. It felt heavy and also natural in her hand. The three stood back-to-back at the ready. Christin and Edith could do nothing to help as they watched on about 25 feet away. Suddenly a flash of bright red light broke the darkness to the right of Rachel's father, Paul. He raised his sword and deflected the blow. Another flash and another deflection.

Out of the rear wall of the chamber emerged another ghostly apparition cloaked in a reddish glow. This apparition was clothed in more elaborate but tattered clothes, resembling the pirate captains of the old movies. A length of rope dangled from his neck. He was twisting and flipping his sword as if provoking the three to attack. Slowly circling the trio. Taunting them, but they stood proud and at the ready awaiting the evil pirate's deadly blows.

"So, you have returned one last time, Benito," Grandfather Wilhem bellowed gruffly at the figure.

The chamber echoed with a deep laugh. "The last time for you, Arvid, old friend. You cursed me to walk this earth without access to my treasure. We have shared this damnation long enough and now you must die one last time so that I might live and regain my fortune."

"Not this time, Bloody Sword. You may have defeated others who have come to battle before me, but together, we three will defeat you and shed ourselves of this eternal fate."

"So, that is how you chose for us to end this then? I send

you and your family to their graves and I continue to walk this earth with my treasure and restored life."

"Not quite. You die and are damned to the depths of the dark abyss and we will find peace."

"Have at it then!" Benito exclaimed as he thrust a mighty blow of his blazing red sword at his once-trusted partner.

Paul struck a counterblow, but Benito was able to easily block it. Rachel swung with all her might at the figure and her sword passed straight through him without making any contact.

"Why didn't that work?!" Rachel exclaimed.

Benito laughed as he replied, "Because you have not fully assumed the vow, young wench. You have answered the call, but you are not yet one of us."

"What do you mean, you old bastard!?"

Benito winked at Rachel and said nothing more. He only smiled and gave an occasional chuckle as they battled on, trading blows. Rachel's attempts were futile and ineffective.

Rachel struggled to find out why she was not one of them until she realized the one thing that made her different. She lowered her sword to her side, closed her eyes, and tilted her head back.

Benito's sword penetrated Rachel's abdomen with a massive impact. In a mighty flash of white light, Rachel became one of them. The light poured from her mortal wound and finally subsided. She stood motionless for a moment and then looked up at Benito as he struck another blow in her direction. This time, Rachel deflected the blow and returned with her own counter to his left shoulder. The blow went deep, and she could feel the tip of her sword impact the bone as it tore through muscle and flesh. A bright red glow began to flow from Benito's wound.

"AAAAAARRRRGGGHH!" Benito screamed. "I see you

have now become one of us, and like us, you are now cursed to the end."

"Not cursed, Benito! BLESSED! Now, die like you are meant to."

"You don't understand. You and your family cannot kill me. Your fight is a futile one."

Benito struck another blow and caught Wilhem in the calf, sending him to his knees. Paul blocked a thrust from Benito as Rachel lined up for another attack. She noticed that Benito's wounds were healing mere seconds after they were inflicted. It seemed their attempts to end the curse were for naught.

Rachel and Paul both hit Benito from opposite sides, causing deep wounds as Wilhem thrust his sword deep into Benito's chest. Benito fell to his knees and bowed his head. A low muffled laugh was heard through the cavern as it echoed off the walls and grew louder. Benito flung his head back in rumbling laughter as he knelt among them. "It is not only your legacy that must fight this battle but mine as well. I told you, you cannot kill me."

Suddenly a familiar voice could be heard screaming from the passage behind Edith and Christin. "They can't, but I can!"

A figure burst from the passage between Christin and Edith and headed across the stream.

"I give myself to Yemayá, and I will serve the sea with all my strength!" the figure shouted.

The figure brandished a sword in its right hand. Once it crossed the stream, the figure glowed with brilliant violet light. It thrust its sword deep into Benito's heart and clean through his body.

Benito doubled over and fell to his side on the smooth battle-worn rock. His red glow began to fade, and he took on a solid form. Blood ran from his wounds and into the stream, tingeing it a bright red in the dim moonlight.

The violet figure stared down at Benito. "I end this now, Grandfather. I relieve this family and ours of this curse. You will haunt us, no more. Our obligations end here."

With Benito's last breath he formed only a single word as he raised his trembling hand toward the figure that had inflicted the mortal blow: "Maria."

Benito's body slid slowly down the smooth rock and into the brisk stream where it was carried over the edge and into the dark abyss below to join the bodies of the ones he had doomed so many years earlier. He would now suffer his fate in eternal damnation.

Rachel looked at the brilliantly lit figure. She approached and embraced her. She whispered softly, "Thank you, Maria."

A soft strain of choral music began to fill the chamber as the four gathered in the pale moonlight.

Wilhem spoke. "Rachel, I must leave you now to find my peace. I will guide you home and Odin's messengers will accompany you. There is a small chest hidden among the treasure. You may take only what will fit inside of it and no more. Do not remove the contents within. Give those things to my dear granddaughter, Gwen. She will know what they are." Wilhem's figure faded from sight and was forever lost to the moonlight.

Rachel turned to her father. "Dad, I cannot claim the treasure. I carry the same curse as you and I cannot leave this place."

"I know, my dear. You have friends who are family to us. They may take your grandfather's portion of the treasure as he instructed."

The fourth figure approached them both. "But you will return home, Rachel. I have been cursed to this island for so long that I have grown to love it and call it home. I have no more family to care for and no one to love. I have had a good life and I owe an obligation to you, this island, my family, and Yemayá. My premonitions are now coming full circle and I, like you, must make a sacrifice to the sea. Your family has endured great torment due to the actions of my great-grandfather and my obligation means I must repay the debts of my ancestors to end this curse. There must be balance."

Rachel gave her a puzzled look. "What do you mean?"

Maria walked to the stream and stood in the middle. "I must pay the debt my grandfather made. You sacrificed yourself out of love and I now do the same. I give myself that you may live for the ones you love."

Rachel screamed, "NO! It isn't yours to give!"

Maria thrust the dagger she had been concealing deep into her chest and collapsed onto it up to the hilt. She rolled onto her side with her hand still clutching the handle of the dagger. A tear ran down her cheek as her brilliant violet glow faded to blackness, leaving only her mortal corpse in a heap in the middle of the chamber. They watched in the dim moonlight as her body followed the same path down the slippery rock into the stream, disappearing into the darkness with a mighty splash echoing from the pool below.

Rachel turned and embraced her father, burying her face in his chest. She sobbed inconsolably. Paul placed his arms around her. "Rachel, it is time for you to go."

"I can't. I can't leave without you."

"You must. I still have work to do, and our obligations have been fulfilled. The sacrifice given that you may live must now be honored and you cannot remain here in this realm or you too will be condemned to the unholy abyss. You will never be alone even though I must soon pass on out of this world, never to return. Your grandfather and I will live forever in you and will guide you just as we always have. Just as this stone floor has been worn smooth by the many battles that have played out upon it, we will continue to fight and protect you so that we may smooth your path, provide you guidance, and give you hope when you need it most; but now it will be through the lessons you have learned and the instincts and abilities passed down to you as a Kristiansen."

Christin and Edith comforted each other near the outer passage. Edith caught a slight glint in the corner of the chamber and broke away from Christin. Under a small outcropping near the floor was the edge of a single gold coin, barely visible. Edith pulled on it, but it would not budge. She pulled at the rock above the coin and it gave way. She started pulling at the rocks around the opening created by the first rock until she had revealed the chamber dug out by the young crewmen of the *Relampago* when the curse first began. In the crevice behind the rock wall was a small trove of treasure and on top of it was a small wooden box similar to the one Rachel had found in Gwen's attic.

Paul began to slowly push Rachel away. "Go now, it is time for you to leave before you are trapped here forever with no way to go back or move on. I will be along shortly."

"Okay, Daddy. Promise me you will follow me."

"My dear, I will always be with you." He gave her a kiss and a strong embrace.

Rachel turned toward Christin and walked back across the stream. Her yellow glow evaporated slowly, and she once again assumed a solid form. She now had a long scar resulting from the penetration of Benito's sword. A scar that would forever be a reminder of her obligations and the sacrifices made for love and family. She turned back toward her father just in time to catch a glimpse of him fading into the darkness as the final shadows of moonlight began to fade from the chamber.

"Daddy, don't go!" she yelled as tears streamed down her face.

Suddenly the dive lanterns began to glow once more as the moonlight faded away. The sudden burst of lantern light surprised the unsuspecting women, leaving them with an uneasy feeling.

Christin held Rachel close while Edith followed the old mariner's instructions and filled the small chest with whatever it could hold. She closed the lid and turned back toward Christin. In doing so, she inadvertently kicked a small rock near the pile of coins causing them to break loose and slide into the current of the stream to be lost to the darkness of the abyssal pool forever. The remaining treasure clanked and rattled through the darkness as the swift waters washed the brilliant gold coins from view. This was the price to be paid to the sea in a bargain struck so long ago.

Edith joined the others and together they made their way back through the passage into the other chamber. Once in the chamber, they noticed glowing light sticks lying on the ground which formed a trail that led them behind a rock outcropping. It seemed that Major Maria Aroza had known about this place and her ultimate fate for a long time. She spent years of service here as a ranger to find and reveal the hidden passage and chamber that were lost to time. She carried the burden of her great-grandfather's curse and embodied the only means to defeat it. She protected the cursed contents in preparation for the day when she could be released from her own unearthly obligations. Unknown to Rachel, it was always a shared obligation between her and Rachel to end the curse. So many souls had been tied together through the ages by a common destiny. In her final act, the major had left a trail of light sticks to lead the trio back to safety.

The women squinted as they made their way out of the cave through a mass of hanging vines and into the bright light of the full moon, emerging at the overlook they had visited earlier in the day with Maria. Rachel was overwhelmed when she realized that they had been so close to the treasure and their destiny but were denied access until they had transcended the trials set forth before them to ensure their worthiness. Maria had known all along but she could not help them for fear of undoing all that had been accomplished through the trials they had endured. Her dutiful silence helped to assure Rachel's success and end the terrible curse Benito's greed had suffered upon his family and the obligations Odin had placed on Rachel and her family.

Rachel surveyed her surroundings to find a path down to the water's edge. Her gaze met the light of the moon and silhouetted against it were the figures of two ravens whose feathers were as dark as the blackest night. They sat silently perched on a weathered branch of a nearby tree. With barely any motion, they observed the events unfolding below. Rachel blew a kiss toward the two visitors from another realm and whispered to them, "Thank Odin for watching over us and guiding us to our destiny." Rachel glanced down for only a few seconds to grasp her gear before once again casting her eyes toward the moon only to find that the ravens had departed without a sound.

They dragged their dive gear along a narrow trail along a rock outcropping and down an incline to the tiny beach below. They suited up for the return swim in silence. With the small chest and its contents suspended from a rope lashed to their buoyancy control vests, they entered the water and swam the 300 feet back to the *Lady Destiny*. Now when their heads were submerged there was no song, there were no headaches; there was only a hushed peace and the sound of water lapping against the rocks. It was an eerie and unsettling silence after enduring the pain and torment of the Sirens' song for so long.

The next morning several rangers approached the *Lady Destiny* and tied up alongside her. A ranger that they had not met before greeted the three as they emerged from the berthing area where they had been sleeping only moments earlier.

In broken English, he introduced himself as Lieutenant Garcia. He was the commander of the second ranger station on the other side of the island. He informed the women that the body of Major Aroza had washed ashore and that it appeared she had stabbed herself in the chest. He also informed them that they had found a suicide note in her bunk and they would be quarantining the sanctuary to allow for a proper investigation. He informed them that the rangers had revoked their permit to anchor and they would now have to leave within the next four hours.

Rachel acknowledged the order and the three broke down in tears. The ranger bid them safe travels and returned to his patrol boat. At the last moment, he paused and turned back toward Rachel. "By the way, Major Aroza stated in her note that I was to give this to you. I'm not sure why, or what it means, but she wanted you to have it." He reached into his pocket and produced a small envelope which he handed to Rachel.

Sobbing, Rachel responded, "Thank you. I appreciate your bringing this to me. We really liked the major and her team. We will pray for her. We will depart within the next couple of hours, once we have gotten everything ready for the open water transit. Goodbye, Lieutenant Garcia."

Lieutenant Garcia waved as he departed their ship and roared away in his patrol boat. Rachel opened the envelope as the patrol boat sped off around the edge of the island. She removed the contents to reveal a list of recipes from the morning meal they'd shared the day before and a map of the caves and buried treasure on the island. Folded up in the center of the papers was another pendant just like Rachel's that appeared to be cut from the same geode as the pendant she wore around her neck. Rachel put the pendant around her neck next to the other one. They fit together in a perfectly matched set. She said to the others, "Imagine spending one's life to right a wrong, to protect a legacy, and sacrifice everything to put things right. This is a far greater deed than anything I could ever accomplish."

Edith went below to check the engines and service the ship's systems while Christin made breakfast. Rachel plotted their course and entered the information into the autopilot and digital mapping system.

After completing their pre-transit preparations and securing everything in its place, Rachel settled back into her chair and pushed the throttles forward as they began their long trek home. This time there was no accompanying music from the Sirens and no headaches, only the low muffled drone of the big diesel engines.

The only other time Rachel had felt so alone was when her father died and she was consumed by emptiness at her loss. It was an uneasy and unwelcome feeling for her. She would no longer have her guiding spirits accompanying her on her treks to sea, or the smells of vanilla and cinnamon to reassure her that everything was going to be all right. It was something she would have to accept and come to terms with, but she was happy in knowing that the torments that had plagued her family were now over and they could all find peace.

Many days later….

Chapter 26

FAREWELL TO FAMILY

Dusk was just settling over the harbor as Edith and Christin attached the last of the shore services to the *Lady Destiny*. Rachel emerged onto the main deck and proceeded to the dock. "You girls good to go?"

"Yeah, get outta here. We'll be along in a minute. Christin just needs to figure out how to get the freshwater strainer on the shore rig unclogged. I wish people would keep these things clean. We hate having to clean them every time we hook up."

"Okay, Edith. I'll see you both tomorrow, thanks for seeing this thing through and making this trip, you know…."

"Enough with the mushy stuff already; go see Gwen before I kick you off your own boat."

Rachel turned and started the short walk to the head of the dock and up the street to Gramma Gwen's house, clutching her small but heavy box. As she approached the rugged home she knew so well, she could see that the lights were on and the windows were open to let in the cool evening air. She could tell there was a fire in the fireplace by the shadows dancing like marionettes on the curtains. When she was a few feet away she could hear a voice speaking, talking directly to Gwen. Of course, Rachel decided to eavesdrop.

"I told you she would be the one to solve the puzzle and put things right. She is smart and strong just like you. I just wish I could have been the one, but you and the others were right to choose her. She is the one we all needed for this."

After a brief pause, the voice started in again. "I know that, and you know she loves you. She thinks about you every day. You don't need to watch over her anymore. She is a woman of incredible means and fortitude. Just love her as she has always loved you."

There was another brief pause. During the interlude, Rachel quietly unlatched and opened the front door a few inches to peer inside. She could see Gwen sitting in her chair leaning forward with her right hand outstretched. At the end of her hand was what appeared to be the hand of a ghostly blue apparition. In most normal circumstances this would send a person into full-on panic at the sight, but oddly it caused her no fear. Gwen began to speak again.

"Yes, I know she has docked and is on her way here. I even suspect she is standing at the door right now. This is your chance to say your goodbyes. Then you must go and find your peace. You have done your job. It is time to move on and be with the rest of those whom you loved and miss. I'll miss you, son. Our time together through the years has meant a lot to me."

Rachel quietly and cautiously entered the room as the apparition turned to face her. The features were not well defined in the fine ectoplasmic mist, but she knew immediately who it was. With its free hand it made a motion as if blowing her a kiss and in an instant, it was gone. Gwen dropped her hand and bowed her head as tears ran down both cheeks. She turned her head toward the door as she wiped the tears away.

Rachel stood in the open doorway as tears ran down her own tanned cheeks and stained her shirt. She could muster only a few words for the spectacle before her. "Goodbye, Daddy. You were always there for me and I love you." At that moment, a cool breeze blew past her and out the door. The odor of vanilla and cinnamon overwhelmed her senses and brought her comfort. She closed her eyes and let the feelings wash over her in a flood of emotions. It felt as if a great energy passed through her, removing her fear and infusing her soul with strength. She knew her guide and protector of so many years was now gone forever.

After a few brief seconds, Gwen got up from her chair and walked as quickly as she could to the door and hugged Rachel as hard as she could. "Welcome home, Rachel. I missed you and I love you so much." Gwen then pulled away as if nothing had happened in a well-rehearsed exercise which she had performed many times before. She told Rachel, "Come in and close the door, my dear. Would you like a hot cup of tea? I just made it."

"That sounds great, Grams," Rachel replied, as she wiped the tears from her eyes.

"Take a chair while I bring the tea, then you can tell me all about your adventures."

"That could take all night."

Gwen looked at Rachel as she poured the tea, "I hope so, honey, I have nothing but time and every moment with you is precious to me, so I don't want to waste any of them." At that moment, the mantle clock began to chime, and the small cottage became awash in the warmth, joy, and emotion of years past. It was a warmth that permeated every nook and cranny and could never be driven out, even by the harshest winter Nor'easter or foulest character.

"I brought you a little something that I think you'll like and by the way, Great Grandad says hello and he loves you."

"That is so nice to hear, Rachel. I wish I could have met him. I suspect that he and your father sent me a little something to lead me to them when it is time for my next big adventure." Gwen's face shown with the light of renewed vigor and a smile was permanently etched upon her lips. She brought Rachel her tea and they both settled back in their chairs in front of the fire for a long, cool night together. They shared stories of love and loss, trial and triumph, pain and sorrow. All they had now was each other, but then that was all they ever really needed.

Until the next quest…

ABOUT THE AUTHOR

Brian R. Langhoff was raised in a small town in Wisconsin and currently lives in North Carolina with his wife, Rebecca. He is active in many civic and charitable organizations, serving in several leadership and mentoring roles. He and his family, which includes a daughter, son, and adult grandson, enjoy the Steampunk and Pirate genres and love to dress up and attend events and festivals whenever possible.

Brian served on submarines in the U.S. Navy and is trained in electronics, industrial maintenance, nuclear technology, and industrial automation. He has been recognized as a Thomas Alva Edison-Max McGraw Foundation Scholar and is an accomplished engineer with numerous patents for various medical devices and products. He currently works as an engineer, designing and building machinery and mentoring young engineers when not writing or entertaining.

Brian has been writing professionally since 1989 and his true passions are storytelling and public entertaining. When visiting public events, he will often appear as one of his many uniquely themed character personas that he has developed over the years. Along with these characters, he has spun numerous tales capturing both the child and the adult imaginations. His writing includes poems, plays, skits, short stories, and essays to entertain readers of all ages and interests. *Return to Cocos*, his sequel to *Cocos Beckons: The Curse of Yemayá* is coming soon.

www.ingramcontent.com/pod-product-compliance
Lightning Source LLC
Chambersburg PA
CBHW050256110726
47898CB00007B/2436